BEGINNING
to Feel the
Magic

BEGINNING
to Feel the
Magic

Linda R. Weltner

Little, Brown and Company

BOSTON   TORONTO

FIRST EDITION

Library of Congress Cataloging in Publication Data

Weltner, Linda.
  Beginning to feel the magic.

  SUMMARY: A sixth-grader experiences emotional highs and lows during a year filled with a class play, a sudden illness, a baby sister, and a boyfriend.
  [1. Family life — Fiction. 2. School stories]
I. Title.
PZ7.W46857Be   [Fic]   80-28057
ISBN 0-316-93052-0

Designed by Susan M. Sherman

BP

*Published simultaneously in Canada
by Little, Brown & Company (Canada) Limited*

PRINTED IN THE UNITED STATES OF AMERICA

Contents

Contents

BEGINNING
to Feel the
Magic

To Lillian Parent
for the time

To Ward Gamble
for the space

And to Julie
for all her loving help

CHAPTER ONE

A Break in Routine

I'm a very emotional person. For a while I thought everyone was, but the older I get, the more I see the difference
between me and normal people.

For example, there were thirty-one of us sitting at desks
in a broken-down building the School Department was always threatening to condemn, and I bet I was the only one
who cared that it was the second day of spring and the windows were closed. And dirty. On the Current Events bulletin board, John Glenn was still in ecstasy about being the
first man in space. He'd been given the chance to circle the
earth and expand his brain while I felt as if a slug had
crawled into mine and filled up the space where I used to
think. Sometimes school can be so stupefying, you get more
stupid every day.

Stupefying. That's one of my father's words and it means
"robbed of your senses." My father always says use a word

three times and it's yours, so here goes. Having to do nineteen almost identical long-division problems after getting the first one right is stupefying (1). It is also stupefying (2) to stop after the fourteenth problem and stare at the wall, trying to decide whether the stains from a leak look more like two butterflies or a man trying to kill a bear with an ax.

I finished four more examples before I began wondering how R.L.D. carved his initials in my desk without getting caught. I made a nice clean frame around the letters, rubbing the dirt off with my finger, which reminded me of Aladdin polishing his magic lamp. I should have remembered how dangerous wishing can be. Every fairy tale has the same moral — the person gets his wish, but he gets something he didn't wish for too, as if it were important for little kids to find out early that there's a dark side to every dream. I wished something special would happen to me, and then I forgot all about it because Miss Latta, the principal of Ash Street School, came into the room.

Miss Latta had on one of those quiet smiles she wore even when she was trying to be serious. She winked at Mrs. McKay when she came in the door, and that meant they'd planned something together. Then she came to the front of the room and stood near my desk, waiting for everyone to pay attention. The tips of a yellow scarf rested perfectly on the shoulders of her navy blue dress so that she looked as if she had wrapped a lily around her neck. She even smelled like a flower.

I was glad I was sitting in the front row. I'd loved Miss

Latta ever since I'd brought a note to the office when I was in first grade and heard her talking on the phone.

"I intend to see that these kids get the best because they deserve it," she'd been saying to someone before I knocked to let her know I was there. We didn't have a library in school so she'd set up a book corner in her office and filled it with books she'd collected on her own. If it had been up to her, we'd have gone on a field trip every day.

My mother's cousin Adele calls Ash Street "a slum school," but the best part about it was that there were only six classrooms in it. Every single teacher knew your name and remembered you all the way back to first grade. You had to go up two flights of stairs to get to the sixth grade and the bathrooms were in the basement, but cruddy green paint and carved-up desks didn't bother me that much. The school felt like a big family sometimes, and kids need that, especially if their own families don't feel like families. And that's something I know a little about. Besides, except for Miss Petra, who cried if you talked back in third grade, the teachers were pretty good. You just had to look at Miss Latta to see that she could have been principal of any school in the whole city of Worcester. Or the state of Massachusetts, for that matter.

"I have good news this morning," she began. "Brookhouse Van Lines has offered us some cardboard wardrobe boxes." She glanced at Mrs. McKay, who was smoothing her short gray curls. Mrs. McKay tried to do so many things at once that she buttoned her blouses crooked and

5

lost her earrings halfway through the day. You wouldn't have thought she noticed, but she did, because the minute Miss Latta walked in, she started trying to fix herself up. I didn't bother to hide my chewed-up fingernails. I gave up on my looks a long time ago.

"When we cut the boxes apart and lay them flat, they will make a perfect backdrop for a class play," Miss Latta continued. A boy in the back whistled. All we'd ever done in school programs was sing or recite poetry. The sixth grade had never put on a play as long as I'd been in school.

"The play we've chosen is *Snow White and the Seven Dwarfs*. We'll need people onstage, but there's a lot that goes on behind the scenes. We'll need costume makers, artists to make posters and programs, people to paint the scenery, ushers . . . Have I forgotten anything?" she asked Mrs. McKay.

"Someone will have to make sure we have all the props, and how about a prompter in case anyone forgets the lines. And makeup," Mrs. McKay said. "They don't call a play a production for nothing."

"Which is why we've chosen you," Miss Latta said in such a personal way that it seemed as if she were talking to only one special person. Me. But I bet every kid in the room felt exactly the same way.

"If we didn't have confidence in you, Mrs. McKay and I wouldn't have dared suggest something this difficult, even for the oldest students in the school. We feel that we can count on you and we hope you'll make us proud of you.

Anyway," Miss Latta went on, since none of us had disgraced her yet, "I stopped by to tell Mrs. McKay that the cartons have been delivered. Mr. Chamberlain, who is head of the high-school art department, has promised to outline the sets this weekend, and as far as I can see, you can begin work Monday morning." She walked to the door, then stopped. "From here on, it's up to you."

The minute the door closed behind her, everyone started talking at once.

"Can I be in it?"

"Who gets to paint the scenery?"

"Can I help?"

A boy named Donald put up his hand and began whining, "Me, me, me, me."

"Wait a minute!" Mrs. McKay's wrinkles usually went all over the place, but this time they all turned down. "Everyone will be part of this one way or another, so quiet down. We're going to hang the cardboard from the walls of the storage room across from Miss Latta's office on the second floor, and those of you who have finished your assignments may go down and work until I send for you. Working on scenery is a privilege you have to earn every time you go down there. It is not an excuse for fooling around. Is that clear?"

Kids nodded who hadn't done anything but fool around from the day they entered school.

"I've gotten hold of some *Snow White* picture books that you can use if you want to go into more detail than Mr.

Chamberlain's sketches. They're here if you want to look at them." Mrs. McKay pointed to a pile of books on the corner of her desk.

Frances, my best friend, put up one hand. With the other, she took off her glasses. When the frames broke, her mother fixed them with a big blob of white tape that sat right on her freckled nose, and now Frances thought they made her look cross-eyed.

"Who can be in it?" Frances asked in her loudest voice. She was working on getting over her shyness.

"There are a lot of parts in this play. Seven dwarfs, a queen, a huntsman, a prince, and Snow White, of course. Then there are smaller parts, ladies-in-waiting, companions to the prince. How many of you would like to be onstage?"

About half the class raised their hands. I raised mine. So did Frances.

"Well," said Mrs. McKay, looking us over. "I think we'll have enough parts to go around."

"When's it gonna be?" Nick called out from the back row. Mrs. McKay seemed pleased to see him showing an interest. She got up from her desk and walked around behind him before she answered. Nick was not a great student, but he did have one special talent. He was the only kid in the class who had figured out how to spend all day lying down at his desk without falling out of his chair. He stretched his legs out under the seat in front of him and hooked his feet on the metal desk legs. I turned around. I could see all of Mrs. McKay. All I could see of Nick was his head.

8

"We have four weeks," she said. "We're going to put the play on right before Easter vacation, the day before Good Friday. We'll put it on for every class in the school Thursday morning. That night, there'll be a performance for the parents. That means we have to start right away and our first job will be to write our own script. How many of you know the plot?"

This time almost every hand went up. Nick put his up and then took it down. Mrs. McKay peered down at him.

"I seen the movie," he mumbled.

"Well, that's fine," Mrs. McKay said. The bell rang for lunch.

I pulled out the peanut butter and jelly sandwich I'd made that morning and ate half of it before the milk cartons got handed out. Mrs. McKay was so worried about food fights, she didn't allow any talking at all. Even the slowest eaters in the room gulped their food down in fifteen minutes.

"Row one," Mrs. McKay called out. Kids filed out a row at a time, dropping empty sandwich bags into the wastebasket. Once they hit the door, there was the usual mad scramble.

"You coming, Julie?" asked Frances, pulling on her ponytail to move it up the back of her head.

I wanted to stay behind and tell Mrs. McKay that I'd give anything if she'd pick me for Snow White, but I couldn't just go up and say, "Give me the best part." That would be like shooting your hand up and down and yelling, "Me, me, me, me." It was Mrs. McKay's job to choose the most beautiful girl in the room for Snow White, which left me out. I didn't think I was ugly, but as Cousin Adele always says, I was born with a boy's nose. I also had bushy eyebrows I was afraid to pluck, and I was taller than most of the boys in the room.

So I went outside with Frances.

I decided not to say anything unless Mrs. McKay tried to make me a dwarf.

CHAPTER TWO

Born to Paint Scenery

When Frances and I came out the door, the other two members of our foursome were waiting for us. Gloria was one of the stars of the YWCA basketball team and she was running in place in the basketball sneakers she wore on the days she had practice after school. Shirley, who's the youngest of eight children, was thumbing through one of the movie magazines she kept in her desk.

Shirley had changed over the summer. When she came back to school, she had to shave under her arms and up her legs all the time, plus she'd filled out on top. A lot. It also affected her personality when her sister Rita got engaged at Christmas to a boy named Sonny who practically moved into their apartment. He started paying Shirley to go to the movies afternoons when her mother was working at the beauty parlor. Shirley must have seen one movie too many because pretty soon she had a crush on just about every movie star you could name. She wrote fan letters in school all the time and scribbled things like *Mrs. Pat Boone* all over her papers. That wrecked her grades and got her moved back to the slow group. Gloria, Frances, and I got to work together in class a lot, but this was our first chance to talk to Shirley all day.

"We decided Joyce will get Snow White," Shirley groaned. "I wish I didn't look so Italian. What do you think Sophia Loren does about the hair on her arms?"

"Some people are born to win and some are born to lose," said Gloria, bouncing up and down. "We decided Joyce was born to play Snow White."

"Snow White's got black hair. You could play her, Shirley. And who says Joyce wants the part anyway?" I asked. Joyce may have been the prettiest girl in the room, but she wasn't exactly the sweet, innocent type. I couldn't picture her keeping house for seven little dwarfs. She'd hire a maid. Or die first.

"She'll want it all right, unless she thinks it's a step down for someone with her looks to play a princess," snorted Gloria.

"Gloria," said Frances, who always defends the underdog, "Joyce can't help her looks."

"Frances." Gloria came to a complete stop. "Joyce does nothing but help her looks. She's got so much practice looking in mirrors, she could play the queen without going to rehearsals."

Gloria usually laughed at her own jokes, but this time she didn't. I wondered if secretly she wished she could be Snow

White, the way I did. Gloria's black, and just for a second, that made me feel funny. I mean, if I felt I couldn't be Snow White just because of my nose . . .

Frances interrupted my thoughts. "If I was Mrs. McKay, I'd make Joyce Snow White. She's so pretty everyone in the audience will understand why the queen picks on her."

Gloria stared at the white knob on Frances's glasses. "Like I'm doing, you mean? You think I'm picking on Joyce because I'm jealous?" She shook her head so hard that some of her tiny pigtails flew loose. "That's a joke. I wouldn't play Snow White if they paid me. They give me the starring role, they got to call this play *No White!*"

She put back her head and started laughing so hard she fell back against the school doors, and that made Shirley start laughing like a maniac. She sat down on her magazine and crossed her legs to keep from wetting her pants. Her sweater pulled up so much you could see her stomach.

"They could give me the lead," Shirley finally got out, "except then they'd have to call it *Slow White.*" Gloria sank down next to Shirley, and the two of them sat there, laughing and wiping the tears off their cheeks.

I looked over to where Joyce was standing against the schoolyard fence, one foot back against the metal screening. She was wearing a pink and gray pleated skirt with a hot-pink sweater under a navy jacket. In one hand, she was holding a tiny zipper case where she kept a comb and rouge. The rest of us got our hair cut by our mothers, but at Christmas Joyce got her hair "shaped," like Jackie Kennedy's, she said, and it fluffed out in a dark cloud all around her heart-shaped face. That was one of her Christmas presents.

The second was that her mother had signed her up with a modeling agency. Standing there, she already looked like a picture in a magazine, except it was a picture of a girl standing all by herself. According to Joyce, she "didn't have time for girl friends."

"Let Joyce be Snow White, if she wants to. Who cares?" I said. "We can work on the scenery. You heard what Mrs. McKay said. We can get out of class whenever we want and be on our own. I'd rather do that anyway."

"Even if Alan's the prince?" Shirley asked.

"What did you and Gloria do, decide who was going to get every part?" I wished I'd never told anyone I had a crush on Alan.

"He's the cutest boy in the class and you know it, Julie. Who else are they going to pick out of the rest of those babies?" The way Shirley said it, you could tell she'd moved on from boys to men.

I tried to change the subject. "How about Nick for the prince? After all, he saw the movie."

"You're full of good ideas today," said Gloria. "He'd be great if the prince didn't have to say a word. He could just about manage to walk onstage. I know. We could write the script so that when Snow White kisses him, he turns into a frog."

"We could write the script so that at the end the prince kisses all the people who painted the scenery. Come on," I begged, "I want us to work on the scenery together."

"You three go ahead," said Shirley. "You always get your work done." She didn't have to say the rest: that we were in the top reading group and she wasn't; that half the time she didn't pass in her homework; that she'd be lucky if Mrs. McKay let her out of class to go to the bathroom let alone paint scenery.

"The only thing wrong with your grades is that you daydream all the time," I said. "We'll come over after school and help you work ahead."

"I don't want to."

"Why not?"

Shirley pulled the magazine out from under her and stared at the cover, so Gloria answered for her. "Her mother's letting her go to the afternoon shows at the Rialto. Sonny's treating."

"Shirley, you can go to the movies, or we can work it out so we can be together in school. What's more important?"

"Lover Come Back," said Gloria. "She wants to see Doris Day twist Rock Hudson around her little finger."

"That's stupid," I said.

"It's not so stupid," said Shirley. "You won't think it's stupid when Snow White over there ends up with Alan crazy about her while you're painting cardboard boxes."

I started to say something, but I'd said too much already, like telling Shirley I liked Alan in the first place. When Alan first transferred into our class right after Thanksgiving, Mrs. McKay told us that his mother had been killed by a drunk driver. I thought he'd be quiet and serious and make us feel as if we were walking near a grave-yard, but he was full of mischief, with long black eyelashes and bangs that kept falling in his eyes. He wasn't hard to talk to at all.

He didn't try to make people like him, but he was curious, the way puppies are, and so interested in people that he was never shy or uncomfortable, even with girls. Wherever he was, something was sure to happen. I should know. One part of me sat at my desk while the other part kept track of every move he made. Like now.

Out in the schoolyard there were some boys playing Chase, using the giant maple tree in the middle of the schoolyard as the jail. Joyce was still by the fence, and Alan was this side of the swings, shifting his weight from one foot to the other. He tugged on his baseball cap.

When I looked at him, he was watching me. He didn't turn the way boys usually do if you catch them staring. Gloria and I were the only two girls who ever played Chase with the boys, so I thought he was checking to see if we were coming into the game. Then he waved his hand, pointing it toward himself, meaning "Come on." I could tell he'd been trying to catch my attention. My cheeks started to burn up.

"I'm going to play Chase. Want to come?" I asked, but Gloria shook her head. Frances had settled down next to Shirley to hear the latest Hollywood gossip.

"Say hello to Alan for us," Shirley called out loud enough for the whole school to hear, but I was already running.

"I'm in," I shouted to the kid who was guarding the jail,

but I really wasn't paying attention to the game. I was wondering if Alan was still watching me. I had just about made up my mind that Mrs. McKay would never put a real kiss at the end of a sixth-grade play when Donald, the "me-me" kid, tagged me from behind.

I headed for jail, which was fine with me. It gave me a chance to watch Alan. Donald was after him now and he was darting from side to side, trying to get away. Both knees on his pants were ripped and his sneakers looked as if a dog had been chewing on them. Alan lived with his father's family now and it seemed as if none of them had noticed that his clothes were falling apart.

It took about two minutes for Alan to give Donald the slip. He stopped to catch his breath. Then all of a sudden he started sprinting in my direction.

I kept one foot on a tree root and reached out my hand. I watched Alan running toward me and his eyes were so dark it didn't look as if he had any pupils at all. I didn't look away until the minute he yelled, "You're free," except that it was more a loud whisper because he was out of breath. I thought he'd tag my hand, but he grabbed it. Then we were running in the same direction, our hands pulling hard against each other at every step.

One. Two. Three.

Then he let go.

CHAPTER THREE

Blood
with a Grin

I didn't dare look at Alan after that, not until we were back in class, and it was his turn to give his science report on blood and blood transfusions. He came up to the front of the room, dumped a clear plastic pouch and some posters on my desk, and knocked all my things onto the floor. He started talking while I was picking pencils out of the aisle, and when I came up again, he was all dimples. It was the first time I ever saw anyone talk about blood with a grin on his face.

The pouch, which had long tubes hanging out of it, was for storing the blood in special refrigerators. The posters showed red cells floating like little doughnuts in the bloodstream. When Alan finished, naturally Joyce asked the first question.

"You look like a doctor with all that stuff. How did you talk them into giving you all that equipment?" Joyce made a trip to the Red Cross office sound like an expedition down the Amazon River. "I'd like to get a better look at those charts, if I could."

"I'm sure Alan will be glad to show everything to you, Joyce," Mrs. McKay said.

"If he hung them on the bulletin board, we could all see them," I suggested.

"Good idea," said Mrs. McKay.

"Good thinking," Frances whispered beside me.

"What's that straw?" Nick asked. He had to come up from under his desk and show Alan what he was talking about. Nick took hold of the tube coming out of the pouch. "Is this where you drink it?"

"Nobody drinks blood. The doctor says, 'Fill 'er up!' and they pump it into your veins like they was filling a car up with gas," a boy named Christopher explained from his seat.

"Shows how much you know," Donald called out. "The Red Cross saves the lady blood for vampires, and if their teeth hurt, they gotta use a straw." A couple of kids in the back started making slurping noises. Mrs. McKay folded her arms and looked strict in their direction.

"I can get blood right out of this vein in my hand," said Walter. This was his second year in sixth grade. A couple of boys stretched out of their seats to see him start pressing the point of his pencil into the back of his hand.

"You're gonna get blood poisoning, you jerk," Christopher announced, standing up. "His blood's gonna turn black as ink. So's his tongue."

"I'm getting sick —" Frances started, but Mrs. McKay cut in with "Thank you, Alan. You may sit down." She put one hand on his shoulder and one on Nick's. It looked like a pat, but it was really a push and it knocked Alan against my desk. She and Nick were already on their way down the aisle toward Walter and kids were scrambling back into their seats.

In the confusion, Alan grabbed one of my pencils with the rest of his stuff. He looked down to make sure I saw him stick it in his pocket. I didn't dare try to grab it back because of what Shirley would say if she saw me get into a tug-of-war with him. I was sure Mrs. McKay was already having second thoughts about what a great class we were. Besides, if Alan wanted my pencil, I wanted him to have it.

I watched him walk back to his seat as if he were on top of the world, and it was funny to know that he was faking it, just the way I did most of the time. That was part of the reason I had a special feeling about him.

I'd never mentioned this to a soul, not even to Frances, but Alan had a funny look in his eyes before he talked to anyone at school in the morning, tired and faraway. He was always kidding around in class as if he didn't have a care in the world, but when he headed home at the end of the day, his shoulders would fall forward and he'd look glad for the hiding place under his hair. It was as if the sadness he brought to school with him got left in the coatroom with his jacket until it was time to put it on again and go home.

I felt we had this secret bond, even if Alan didn't know

it. School seemed like the one place both of us could forget what was bothering us at home.

Anyway, I'd liked him from the minute I saw him, and since that day, I hadn't changed my opinion of him, except in one respect.

I was beginning to think he liked me too.

A truly stupefying (3) thought.

CHAPTER FOUR

Left Out

I wasn't sure my mother would be home after school. She used to work from nine until two at a fancy children's clothing store that Cousin Adele manages. That way she was usually home in the afternoons. After my sister was born, she quit, so I thought she'd be home all the time. But now it seemed as if she needed to get out of the house more — "to keep from eating," she said when I asked her. She'd leave the baby with my grandmother during Hope's afternoon nap, promising to be back by the time school was out, but most of the time she didn't make it. My father once said if she arrived anywhere on time, he'd believe in miracles.

I wanted to tell her all about the play, so I felt lucky to find her in Hope's room, changing the baby's diaper. She was holding the baby's feet in one hand and smearing white cream with the other. She was still wearing slippers and hadn't gotten around to brushing her hair. It looked as if she'd had a bad day.

"Hello, I'm home," I said from the doorway.

"Can you get me a shirt from the second drawer, hon? This one's soaked." I found a white one with "Wonder Woman" printed on the front and brought it over.

"Is this one OK?" I asked. My mother took it without saying thank you. The baby was drooling on the mat and my mother was making little clucking noises to keep her from crying. I stood there, trying not to smell the diaper pail, watching a chunk of milk slide down the saliva running out of Hope's mouth. I could feel the excitement inside me starting to turn sour in my stomach.

"You'll never guess what happened today in school," I said. Even though I knew better than to try and get my mother's attention when she was busy, I couldn't help it. I felt I'd waited too long already.

"Let me put the baby in her high chair." My mother picked Hope up, and the first thing the kid did was to throw up on her shoulder. The gunk made two soggy trails down the back of my mother's red sweater.

"You messy girl. You big drooler," my mother baby-talked. She held the baby away from her and wiggled Hope from side to side. "You spit up on your mommy. You big bum!" The baby laughed out loud. My mother laid her down in her crib.

"What a mess!" My mother wiped her shoulder with a dry diaper. "Let me go change."

I walked over to the crib. Wonder Woman stared up at

me as if I were the most interesting thing she'd ever seen. All at once her face turned meat red and her eyes squashed into slits. She grunted and pushed like a little pig and she was still at it when my mother came back wearing a man's sweat shirt that hid the thirty pounds she'd put on.

"If it isn't one end, it's the other," I said. "You're going to have to change her again."

"Hopey, you are really dopey." My mother picked the baby up and put her back on the changing table. "I don't know which side of the family you take after, but if I ever find out, they're going to be sorry. Sooo sor-ree," she murmured, pushing her face against the baby's neck, and suddenly I couldn't stand to watch the two of them any longer.

"How could you say a dog was too much work?"

My mother twisted around. One hand kept rubbing Hope's stomach. "Sweetheart, when you housebreak a puppy, all you end up with is a pet. When Hope is through this stage, this family's going to have a little person and you're going to have a friend."

"When I'm twenty-two, she'll only be eleven years old."

"Well, you might have to wait until you're a little older. Get me another outfit, will you?"

I figured by the time I was fifty I'd have all the friends I wanted, but I didn't say it. Instead, I went over to the bureau and pulled out a pink shirt and red corduroy overalls. I stood close to my mother while she slipped the legs over the baby's feet.

"I'm sorry," I said. "It's just that I'm trying to tell you what happened at school."

"And I'm trying to listen. With both hands full." She tightened the shoulder straps. Then she pushed at the diaper with the tips of her fingers. "What a mess. I should never have started her on peas."

"Can't you listen for one minute?"

My mother stood up straight and stared at the wall behind the changing table. "It's perfectly normal for you to feel you should be the constant center of attention, Julie, but I don't want to hear about it right now, OK?" She pushed chunks of hair off her face with the back of her hand, but it all fell back.

"You don't want to hear about anything," I said.

"Not when I have a diaper to stick down the toilet, I don't."

"Oooh, I'll be upstairs visiting Bubbie," I said in my most disgusted voice, but my mother was so busy putting Hope back in her crib, she didn't even notice.

I went out into the front hall and up the staircase that led to my grandmother's apartment on the second floor, past old bureaus piled high with cardboard cartons. My grandmother hadn't thrown anything away since the day she'd been forced to leave all her belongings behind in Russia, and that was forty years ago. The upstairs hall was dark and stuffy and it reminded me of the morning I'd crawled into bed with my mother and put my head on her stomach so that I could feel Hope move inside her. It was nice and warm under the covers and I had to lie there a long time, waiting for the baby to cooperate. When she finally kicked, it was like a miracle.

"The baby really outdid itself that time. Showing off for you, I bet," my mother had said, hugging me. That was the last time I felt that four was the right number for a family.

My father's mother opened her door.

"So you're hiding out here," she said. Then she went back into her kitchen. Grandma Hessie wasn't one for asking questions. She and my mother made an agreement that if they were going to live together in a two-family house, they wouldn't interfere in each other's business. My grandmother was very good at it. She almost never came into our apartment.

I went into my grandmother's kitchen, which was about the size of some people's closets. She fit right in, though, because my grandmother, who was shorter than I was, was the size of some people's children. She was bending over a chicken that came from a special butcher my father knew and that still had a few black pinfeathers on it. She bought her chickens undressed, which meant they still had the guts in and she had to clean them out. She threw everything away except for the liver, the giblets, and the unborn eggs. That's the way she'd done it in Russia when she was a bride, and that's how she intended to do it for the rest of her life.

"I have an egg for you," she said. "Open," and she slipped a yolk hot out of the boiling water into my mouth with a spoon. She came over to the table and sat down across from me. She brought a cup of tea without any sugar in it, and before she drank, she took a sugar cube and stuck it into the space under her tongue. That's an old Russian custom my father says rots your teeth.

Sucking on sugar made the two little bumps on the top of my grandmother's head wiggle. She reminded me of the billy goats at Green Hill Park. When I was little, before my father told me they were harmless cysts, I used to think I had the only grandmother in the world who'd started to grow horns.

"Wor pudding on . . ." I started. I took a sip of my grandmother's tea to rinse the yolk from the roof of my mouth, where it was stuck like peanut butter. I wondered whether she'd be interested in something that had happened in America.

"We're putting on a play at school."

"A big girl like you shouldn't play in school."

"Not that kind of play, Bubbie. A play where you learn the lines by heart and then you act it out onstage."

She sipped her tea and nodded.

"The play's called *Snow White*. We're going to put it on for parents and you can come. Did you ever see a play?"

My grandmother spit sugar bits into her saucer. "I seen enough, I don't have to go to a play. Sometimes you have enough excitement, you don't go looking for any more." She was leading up to one of her stories, but this time I had a story of my own to tell.

"The school never had enough money for scenery and costumes before, but somebody gave us stuff and the principal decided to give the sixth grade a chance. I might be in it —"

"So now you want to be a movie star?"

"No, I just want . . ." I didn't know what else to say.

"Your father took me to the movies once. Once was plenty. Feh, let rich people waste their time."

She got up from the table and went back to plucking feathers. "You want a cookie?" Without waiting for an answer, she took down a coffee can that was on top of her refrigerator and held it in front of me. I reached in and took three cookies to eat while I was doing my homework. I didn't even have to look to know that the cookies would be S-shaped and taste like sweet, stale bread even when they were fresh from the oven.

Some things never changed, like my grandmother's cookies, and some things were brand-new and I didn't think I'd ever get used to them.

Like feeling so left out when I came home.

CHAPTER FIVE

Never Say Hello

"Eleanor!"

I was in my bedroom working on math when my father came home. He walked into the kitchen, calling my mother's name in a voice so loud it traveled through the whole house. Nobody in our family believed in starting a conversation by saying hello.

"Eleanor, that thief Costello tried to pull another fast one today. Barney told him we'd give him eight cents a pound profit for lamb's wool and he tried to unload junk on us."

I can guarantee that whatever my mother was doing, she stopped in her tracks. Hope still had a thing or two to learn from my father about getting attention.

By the time I got into the kitchen, my father was on the phone with Barney, the man he worked for in the wool business. His company bought and sold the wool that fell under the machines when they manufactured yarn in the mills. My father once helped me make a beautiful chart of all the different things that happened to wool from the time it left the sheep's back until it became a sweater you put on your own back.

That was B.H. Before Hope.

My father paced back and forth at the end of the telephone, talking so loudly my mother and I couldn't say a word. He was so afraid of getting flabby now that he'd turned forty-five that he never sat still if he could move. It didn't help that he was eating a tomato and talking with his mouth full. My mother finally gave him the signal that dinner was ready.

"Barney thinks Costello's met his match in me," my father continued at the table. He was chewing on a lamb chop, but it didn't interfere with his train of thought. That just kept chugging along the same track. "Barney knows I can beat Costello at his own game."

"Barney knows what you're worth to the business, Hal," my mother said. She'd brushed her hair and put on lipstick. "I know he'd pay it to you. If you'd only say something —"

"Barney wouldn't pay his mother what she's worth. Don't worry, it won't be long before I start my own company. I'll be glad not to owe that skinflint a nickel." My father reached over and stabbed my mother's potato with his fork. "I'll eat that. You're not going to take off weight unless you cut down on starchy foods."

"I happen to be hungry," my mother said very slowly.

"Eat some lettuce. It's better to be hungry than obese."

My mother put down her fork. She put both hands on the table and her knuckles were white. "Since you cooperated in getting me pregnant, I thought we agreed to call my new padding baby fat."

"For God's sake, Eleanor, don't be oversensitive."

"I prefer it to being insensitive."

"I'm eating this for your own good," my father said with his mouth full of potato. "What kind of an answer is that?"

Hope started making whimpering sounds in the bedroom.

"You'll have to excuse me. Somebody wants something for a change." My mother pushed her chair away from the table so hard it would have fallen over if I hadn't grabbed it. My father picked up his lamb chop with his fingers and tore a strip off with his teeth, as if the lamb chop had interrupted his conversation.

I didn't know why my father couldn't seem to figure out that the more he needled my mother about gaining weight, the more sweet stuff she'd haul into the house. I said the first thing that popped into my mind to try to change the subject.

"What's a skinflint?"

"You don't know the word *skinflint?*" My father frowned. "It's someone who's a cheapskate, such a cheapskate he'd take the skin right off you with a sharp piece of flint, the kind of rock they make arrowheads with."

"Then he'd charge you for the operation."

My father laughed. He looked right at me for the first

time since he'd come home. "Very clever." He's always astonished to discover I have a sense of humor. "How about *obese?*"

I poked at my potato so I wouldn't have to answer, but he kept at me. "Fat," I said finally.

"Not just fat, but fat as a beast, like, say, your average two-ton hippopotamus." He smiled at me, lifting up his bushy eyebrows as if he expected me to laugh. My father's pointy ears and eyebrows make him look like a handsome devil, and his jokes can sting as much as being poked with a pitchfork.

I wouldn't smile back. It bothered me that my mother looked as if someone had stuffed pancakes under her cheeks and forehead, but she wasn't ready for the zoo, no matter what my father said. He seemed to think that just because his body looked like a muscle factory, he had the right to make fun of everybody else. Thank God I was born a naturally skinny person.

"A good vocabulary is the key to success," he lectured, getting off on another favorite subject. "I never met a new word I didn't look up in the dictionary. I had to drop out of school, but not having a diploma never held me back because —"

"You developed your vocabulary," I finished.

"You may be tired of hearing it, but some things can't be said too many times."

"Could I tell you something?" I began, but my mother came back and my father had to repeat to her how cleverly I'd used his definition of *skinflint,* and then they started arguing about what time my father would get back from bringing my grandmother to Friday night services.

I watched the two of them and it could have been any night of the week, my father pretending he never had anything to do with getting my mother angry, and my mother so tired and tense that the blue of her eyes was flat and watery. Since Hope, her mouth had shrunk down to tight little lips.

I wanted a chance to tell my mother what had happened at school, but as soon as we'd finished dinner, the phone rang for her. I couldn't help hearing the conversation while I was doing the dishes.

"Of course I saw that in the paper, Adele, but the robbery took place six blocks away." (Cousin Adele went on and on before my mother got a chance to squeeze in a few sentences.)

"No, I am not worried, and yes, I do care, but I am not afraid of my neighbors and I like Julie's friends." (Adele nearly died the first time she saw Gloria.)

"I can't help but think that if God had wanted us to live in a Jewish neighborhood, he would have made the whole world Jewish." (According to Cousin Adele, I should already be looking for someone to marry.)

"In my opinion, Hal is very generous. We'll move when he's got the money — unless *you* want to pay the rent." (When they started in about my father, I left.)

I should have finished my homework, but instead I got into my pajamas and pulled out some photographs I'd taken from albums my mother kept in the living room, pictures of us at the beach or out on our lawn, which is the only stretch of grass in the neighborhood.

My favorite picture showed me brushing my hair out by our picket fence, and the sun made it look like a waterfall of light falling all the way down my back. No one had thought it was a tangle of snarls that needed to be cut short until Hope was born. Behind me, my father was pushing the lawn mower with his shirt off, tipping his face up to the sun. The picture had a quiet, just-right feeling.

All of the photographs were like that, as if we were some other family in some other world. One of the pictures was taken at my grandmother Rachael's house, and it showed my mother and father climbing out of an old Ford. Another showed my parents standing in the waves at Nantasket Beach, swinging me back and forth in the water between them. In all the pictures, my father looked relaxed and friendly, and my mother seemed happy and peaceful and thin. I looked as if I owned the world.

I looked at the pictures and I could feel the closeness. The way that family got along was right there for anybody to see until Hope fell off the tree like a rotten apple and landed in our laps. By being small and helpless, she took over the whole family, *my* family, and ruined it. Somehow she'd made the rest of us sick of each other.

Then my thoughts switched from home to school, and it was as if someone had flipped on a light and made everything bright again.

As clearly as I saw the people in the photographs, I could

see Alan watching me in the schoolyard and feel the place where he'd held my hand. I wondered if we'd get to work on the scenery together, and what he'd do if I tried to get my pencil back.

All those thoughts made me feel lighter and lighter until I felt like a helium balloon that rises straight up in the sky when you let it go, leaving everything else stuck to the ground. I felt lifted up by the excitement swirling inside me, and my mother and father and Hope seemed very tiny and far away, as if they had nothing to do with me at all.

It seemed so simple. They didn't want to know about me, so until the night of the play, I wouldn't tell my parents one single thing about school. I wouldn't even drop hints to try to get them to ask me questions. I'd be a skinflint and keep my life all to myself, and the funny thing was, they wouldn't even know it.

When I finally came home with a notice about the play, my parents would be surprised. They'd be amazed when they saw the scenery and I told them what part of it I'd done. If they asked me why I hadn't said a word, I'd just explain, "I didn't think you'd be interested." After that, they'd always wonder what else was happening in my life that I wasn't telling them.

I made my decision and then I floated off to sleep.

CHAPTER SIX

When It's Once Upon a Time

$\mathcal{M}$onday morning, Mrs. McKay read us the story of Snow White from a big blue book. I remembered it the way Walt Disney made the movie, but it was really written in Germany almost two hundred years ago by two brothers named Jacob and Wilhelm Grimm.

Mrs. McKay asked us a lot of interesting questions about the story, like what did we think had happened to Snow White's father. How come he didn't know his new wife hated his daughter? Or didn't he care?

"It sounded like him and the first queen was real glad to have a baby before she croaked," said Walter. "I bet he was real broke up when the queen died." That made me think of Alan.

"In those days, guys would put on these shiny suits of armor and go have a war, like a king would go off on horses with a bunch of knights and they'd live in these big tents with stripes on them. I seen a movie like that," said Christopher.

"Maybe that's the reason the queen was so jealous," said Frances. "Not just about Snow White's looks, but because the king went away a lot after he married her." Frances's father worked at a gas station during the day. Nights he drove a taxi. That's why her family had just gotten a dog named Bandanna, because Frances's mother was afraid to stay home alone at night.

"You could almost feel sorry for the queen," said Shirley.

"How could you feel sorry for somebody who would eat your liver?" asked Donald.

"Not the liver," Mrs. McKay corrected him. "The queen asked for Snow White's heart."

"I bet the queen thought the king married her for her looks, and only the most beautiful woman in the world could hold on to him," said Joyce. "I bet she thought he was cheating on her."

"I seen this movie where some soldiers raped these girls they captured. They tore the clothes off one of them and she had real big—" Nick began, but Mrs. McKay didn't let him continue.

"Nick, we are discussing the queen's feelings," she warned him.

"I seen that movie. She had real big eyes," said Christopher, moving his eyebrows up and down as if he were saying something dirty.

"How could a grown woman hate a young girl?" Mrs. McKay asked, ignoring them both.

"Maybe the queen wanted all the king's money for herself," I volunteered.

"I think the queen was really angry at the king for never being home, but since he wasn't there, she took it out on Snow White," Gloria answered.

I knew for a fact that Mrs. McKay once told Gloria that she ought to think about being a psychologist when she grew up because she had such a good understanding of human behavior, but she'd never heard Gloria talk about her mother. According to Gloria, it was never her fault when her mother chased her around the house with a shoe. No matter how fresh she got, she blamed it on her mother's bad mood from a fight with her boyfriend the night before. The two of them had terrible tempers — "short and sweet," Gloria said — but the way Gloria saw it, someone else was always to blame. If Mrs. McKay had asked her, Gloria would probably have said that the wolf had tried to eat the three pigs because Mrs. Wolf had put him in a bad mood.

We were supposed to be talking about Snow White, but all the kids seemed to be talking about themselves.

"What I can't see is why Snow White would want to be like a cleaning lady to a bunch of dwarfs," said a girl named Diane, whose mother worked nights as a nurse. Diane made dinner and put her sisters to bed every night. "How could she like mending and sewing and keeping everything clean? That's what I'd like to know."

"Well, what do you think it was like for Snow White to live in a castle?" Mrs. McKay asked her.

"I bet she never had to lift a finger," Diane answered. "You said she had ladies who waited on her."

"What's so great about that?" asked Walter. "My mother cleans houses for these rich ladies and she's not supposed to talk to their kids or nothin' 'cause she's the hired help. I feel sorry for 'em."

"People who aren't family don't really care," Alan said. "Usually, they have their own children. They just do it for the money."

"Maybe living in a castle was just plain boring," said Gloria. "Nothing to do, no friends to hang around with, a stepmother who spends all her time talking to a mirror."

"Maybe cleaning house for the dwarfs made her feel useful," I said, "if it was the first time in her life somebody needed her."

"What girl wouldn't want to live in a house with seven men?" asked Shirley. "If it was me, I wouldn't care if they made me scrub the toilets."

"You would when you found out they didn't have no plumbing," said Christopher. "You'd be shoveling out the you-know-what."

"That's enough," said Mrs. McKay. "Stand up, Christopher!"

Christopher slowly pulled himself up beside his desk. He started playing with the gold cross gleaming against his dark skin, trying to look holy, which was pretty hard for someone who always wore his shirts unbuttoned all the way down to his belt.

"Is that your idea of a positive contribution to this discussion?" Mrs. McKay used her "you-better-watch-your-self" voice.

"When it's once upon a time, they don't have no plumbing," Christopher said. "I just wanted to give Shirley the right picture of the history of it."

Mrs. McKay reached behind her and picked up the storybook. " 'On a winter's day, many years ago,' " she read. *"Not* 'Once upon a time.' You are the one who had better have the right picture, Christopher. Do you get the picture?"

"Yes, ma'am," he said, folding his tall, skinny self back into his seat.

CHAPTER SEVEN

Deep in
the Dark Woods

*T*hat same Monday, we started work on the scenery. The cardboard was up on the walls of the storage room across from the principal's office, and after a few days, things began to take shape.

After kids finished coloring in Mr. Chamberlain's outlines of trees and branches, they started copying little animals out of the picture books Mrs. McKay got from the library. There were baby birds in nests, foxes, owls, rabbits, and even a deer peeking out from behind a tree. That was one wall, the woods.

If you turned to the opposite wall, you were inside a little cottage with a china cabinet drawn against the wall and two windows with painted curtains. One of the windows was cut on three sides so that it would open when the queen stuck her ugly face in to hand Snow White the apple.

On a third wall, a mirror filled a piece of cardboard that went almost to the ceiling. Mr. Chamberlain had put sheets of aluminum foil down the middle to give the right effect. He'd drawn carved devils all around the mirror frame, and kids had colored all the devils' eyes red to make them look more evil.

The storage room was small and there wasn't too much room to move when more than five or six kids were working. Five of us got a perfect score on the test Mrs. McKay gives every Monday to see who knows the spelling words. For the rest of the first week, we spent the first hour every day working on the scenery. It was a good group — me, Alan, Frances, Gloria, and Christopher, who had written the spelling words on the cuff of his shirt sleeve.

By Friday, we were starting to put in special touches.

Alan drew beautiful black horns on the deer and turned it into a buck.

"Do you think his eyes ought to be red?" he asked. "The woods are dark. Maybe his eyes ought to glow?"

"The hunter's going to try to stab Snow White in the heart right in front of these woods. That ought to frighten the little kids enough, without scaring them to death with red eyes," Gloria answered.

"I think the woods ought to feel kind," I said. "The castle is dangerous, but the woods are safe. I'd rather see brown eyes." That was the way I felt about it.

We all looked into the woods. There were about fifteen animals looking back at us and all of them looked friendly.

"Turn around. What do you think of my dishes?" I asked. I was working on the plates Mr. Chamberlain had outlined in the china cabinet. I drew pink lilies of the valley in the middle and ivy leaves all around the edges. When you stood back against the woods, it looked like real china leaning against the back of the shelf.

"Where do you think the dwarfs bought dishes?" asked Christopher, who was stretched out in a corner with his hands behind his head, watching the rest of us work. "You think they got them at Denholm's, your friendly department store?"

"I didn't think about how they got them," I said. "I should have made them look like clay dishes."

"Don't worry about it," said Frances, who was putting tiny black hearts on the yellow curtains. "Nobody will notice."

Alan came over to look at my dishes.

"If there are kings and queens, there have to be towns where people do their shopping. Somebody would make dishes like those, Julie. I bet they would because those flowers are the kind that grow in the woods. We ought to put some under the trees."

While Alan was talking, Gloria went over and closed the door. Then she turned out the light. There was a window over the door so it wasn't pitch-black, but it was pretty dark.

"It looks real now, doesn't it?" she asked. Light shimmered off the aluminum foil and made shivery streaks on the ceiling. The four of us stood in the middle of the room, looking around.

"What if we opened the door and the school wasn't out there?" Alan asked.

"What would be there instead?" I said.

"More forest."

"I'd go for it," said Christopher from the corner. "We could all live together in this cottage and the girls could wash our socks and cook us dinner."

"The queen wouldn't need to come knock us out with a poison apple," said Gloria. "One whiff of your socks and we'd be out cold."

"Come off it." Even in the dark, you could tell Christopher was grinning. "You know you'd love it. Every time you didn't burn the food, Alan and me would give you a chunk of gold from the mines."

"If Snow White had to live in the woods with guys like you, she'd have run back to the hunter screaming, 'Kill me! Kill me!' " Gloria started yelling.

"You're just hollering 'cause you know the way you cook, you'd never get no gold," Christopher yelled back.

The yelling made me panic. Two more minutes of it and we'd be explaining to Miss Latta why we were painting scenery with the lights off.

"Shut up, Gloria," I said. "We wouldn't have to lift a finger. If we needed anything, we'd just draw a picture."

"Will you please open the door?" asked Frances.

"Why? You think living in the woods with us could be worse than going to school?" Christopher sounded really amazed at the thought.

"It won't do any good to open the door anyway," said Alan, sounding like a voice at a funeral. "The school's gone."

44

I could feel him standing right beside me in the dark even though I was looking straight ahead. Seeing a person without your eyes is like listening to a faraway sound and not knowing where it's coming from. It makes you go real quiet inside. I hadn't even known that could happen.

Nobody said a word. If anyone had knocked at the door right then, we all would have started screaming.

"I want to get out. It's scary in here," said Frances.

"No, it's not," said Alan. "You heard what Julie said. Outside it's dangerous, but the woods are safe."

Christopher started slithering along the floor. We could hear him moving and making a noise in his throat that was a cross between purring and growling.

"Cut it out, Christopher," Gloria ordered. "Frances isn't kidding!"

"Please," whispered Frances. I stuck my hand out behind me and she grabbed hold of it.

"You don't have to be afraid, Frances, ' said Alan, and I don't know how, but I could tell he was looking at me in the dark. "Out there, they'll get you. The rest of us like it better in here."

I don't know what would have happened next if someone hadn't knocked, but she did and we could hear her, even deep in our dark secret woods.

Gloria opened the door and there it was again, right behind Joyce's smile.

Dark oak doors. Green paint. Dirty windows.

School.

CHAPTER EIGHT

Tryouts

*B*y the second week it seemed as if all we did was eat, sleep and dream Snow White. In math, we figured out how much material we needed to make shirts for seven dwarfs. Mr. Van Dusen, who taught German at the high school, showed us slides of German castles and then read "mirror, mirror on the wall" in German. It sounded weird.

In English, we started writing sentences for the characters to say to each other in the play. Mrs. McKay would take a scene, like the one in which the hunter decides not to kill Snow White, and we'd invent what she called "dialogues."

"When the hunter stops in the woods and pulls out his knife, what do you think Snow White might say?" That's one example.

"Are we stopping here for a picnic?" Joyce suggested.

Frances liked, "Why are you doing that? Do you see a wild animal?"

46

It got so I was making up conversations in my head, imagining all the scenes in the play, even dreaming about it at night as if I were under some magic spell. A silly fairy tale began to seem as real as my own life.

On Wednesday of the second week, Mrs. McKay asked how many kids still wanted to act in the play. A lot of hands shot up, but there were quite a few kids like Frances, who was afraid she'd forget her lines if she had too many. Mrs. McKay put a list of characters on the board.

"Let's do the scene with the mirror first," she said. "Who wants to try out for the queen?" At first, nobody moved. Then I raised my hand and so did Joyce. She looked as if she'd come to school dressed for the part. She had on a big pink birthstone ring and tiny rhinestone earrings.

"I'm having you try out in front of the whole class because I want you to get used to performing in front of people right from the beginning. If you concentrate on your lines, you'll forget to be nervous. Joyce, why don't you come up first? All you have to say is 'Magic mirror on the wall, who is the fairest of us all?' Who wants to be the mirror?"

"We already got a mirror," said Nick.

"There has to be someone to stand behind the mirror and say, 'O queen, you are fair, but none to Snow White can compare.' Nick, no one will see you and you can read the lines. Come on and try it." So Nick came up to the front of the room.

Mrs. McKay handed Joyce a mirror with a long handle, the kind movie stars keep next to their perfume bottles.

"When the mirror answers, the queen says, 'That horrible child. We'll see about that.' If you forget the exact words, say anything." Mrs. McKay moved back against the blackboard. Joyce and Nick stood facing each other at the front of the room.

Joyce looked into the mirror. She pulled at her hair and twisted a curl against her cheek. She wet her lips.

"Magic mirror on the wall," she murmured, and smiled so that everyone could see her perfect teeth. "Who is the fairest of us all?"

Nick stood there. He looked at Mrs. McKay. He looked at Christopher, who had his legs up and was sitting in his seat like a grasshopper. He stared up at the ceiling.

"Say anything you want," said Mrs. McKay.

Then Nick looked happy. "Eat your heart out, queen," he burst out. "Snow White makes you look sick!"

"That rotten kid!" Joyce's eyes were flashing. "That horrible child!" She was really good at hate. "Well!" She put her hands on her hips and started tapping one foot very slowly. "I think I'll show her a thing or two." She was perfect in the part. I could imagine her saying the same words when she wasn't even acting.

"OK, Julie, you try it," said Mrs. McKay. I came up front and took the mirror from Joyce. I closed my eyes and took a deep breath so my voice wouldn't shake. I was just ready to start when Mrs. McKay interrupted: "Hold on a minute." There was a girl standing at the door with a note.

When Mrs. McKay went over to talk to her, I looked in the mirror. My cheeks were pinker than usual and my

48

eyes, which are hazel, looked almost green. I realized that when I looked straight at myself, my nose seemed the right size. I didn't look so bad, at least from the front.

"Go ahead, Julie," said Mrs. McKay.

Nick was really getting into his part. "You stink!" he snarled at me. "Snow White's cuter than you any day!"

My part was easy. I thought about Hope. "That spoiled brat! It's time that girl got put in her place."

"Thank you both very much," said Mrs. McKay. "Who wants to be the hunter?"

Christopher's hand shot up like lightning.

"OK, Christopher, come over here. The hunter stops and pulls out his knife. You can use a ruler for now. After Snow White speaks, you say, 'Run away, poor child.' Who wants to play Snow White?" I folded my hands on my desk and looked around.

Gloria raised her hand. She must have thought a lot about it, but she hadn't said a word to me.

"All right, Gloria. Your line is "Oh, dear hunter, don't take my life. I'll run into the woods and never bother you again.' Stand over by the window with Christopher and take a few steps before either of you says anything."

Christopher put the ruler in his back pocket. Then he walked to the front of the room and pulled it out. He sharpened it on his pants leg. He pulled the edge along his finger and said, "Oow!" That was supposed to show how sharp it was.

"Oh, dear hunter," Gloria began. Then she stopped. "That's pitiful."

"She should probably get down on her knees and beg me," suggested Christopher, blowing on his knife blade.

"You can get down on your knees if you want to, Gloria, but let's forget 'Oh, dear hunter.' Just say, 'Don't take my life. I'll run away and never bother anyone again.' "

"I'm not getting down on my knees," said Gloria.

"People always get down on their knees when they're begging for their life. Didn't you ever see no gangster movies?" Christopher always knew how to drive Gloria crazy.

"I'm not going to beg," Gloria said in a voice Mrs. McKay couldn't hear. Her teeth were shut together. Just her lips moved.

"So don't beg," whispered Christopher. "I like liver."

"Gloria," said Mrs. McKay. "I don't care how you do it. Just say, 'Don't take my life.' "

"OK." Gloria stood as tall as she could. She looked straight ahead at Christopher's bare chest and said in her loudest voice, "Don't take my liver!"

"I wouldn't take your liver if you got down on your knees and begged me," said Christopher.

"It's 'Don't take my *life*,' Gloria," Mrs. McKay repeated. "Why does everyone keep thinking it's the liver? The queen wants Snow White's heart."

"I don't want this part." Gloria started walking back to her seat.

"Don't be discouraged, dear. I know you can do it. Try it again."

"I don't want to do it. Snow White's a stupid jerk," said

Gloria, and she sat down. If looks could kill, Christopher would have been a dead man.

"Well?" Mrs. McKay looked around. No one moved. "Diane?"

"If the play's at night, I might not be able to be in it," said Diane. "It depends if the hospital lets my mother off the night shift." She came up and tried, though. I thought she was pretty good. She had a soft voice that made it seem as if any hunter would really feel sorry for her.

"Julie, are you interested in trying out for this?"

I got up and stood beside Christopher. I remembered how he'd gone along with Alan's idea of us all living in the forest together. Gloria thought he only wanted to make fun of us, but I had the feeling he was beginning to feel the magic, too. The way I did.

"Don't take my life," I said, reaching over and pushing his hand with the ruler away. "I'll run into the woods and never come back again. Let me escape and you'll never be sorry. I promise."

"Go ahead," he said, pointing to the door. "You'll be safe in the woods. I'll figure out some way to trick the queen."

"Well, now, that was fine," said Mrs. McKay, stepping forward. She took a deep breath. She had chalk dust all over her jacket. "Who wants to be a dwarf?"

The tryouts lasted until lunch. When we came back in from recess, the list of characters was on the board with a name beside every one. Frances and Shirley were two of the ladies-in-waiting to the queen. They got to carry the mirror on- and offstage, with Nick hiding behind it.

Christopher was the hunter. Gloria was going to be the narrator and introduce the play by telling the history of fairy tales.

Seven boys were the dwarfs. Donald and Walter were going to play the soldiers who carried Snow White's unconscious body offstage on a cot from the nurse's office. They were supposed to drop Snow White's coffin to make her spit up the apple and come back to life. I was right. No kisses.

Joyce screamed when she saw that she was the queen. I guess she'd noticed that the queen had the most lines, plus two costume changes, including a long cape to wear to Snow White's wedding.

Alan was the prince. Mrs. McKay said she would teach him how to waltz for the last scene when he and Snow White got married in front of the whole cast.

I was so nervous I couldn't look at the blackboard. I sat down and stared at my desk and listened to everyone talking at once. Frances had to come over and tell me.

Diane was one of the ladies-in-waiting.

I was Snow White.

CHAPTER NINE

Too Much Excitement

Once the parts were given out, the play got going like a rocket shooting off its launching pad. We started rehearsing in pairs and didn't stop, even at recess. Kids stayed after school to work on props and make costumes with the sewing teacher from the high school. I was going to wear a long pink skirt with a ruffle at the bottom. Mrs. McKay suggested that I take it home over the weekend and practice walking in it, but Frances took it to her house instead. I went baby-sitting with Frances Saturday night and we flounced around in our long skirts and went over my lines until I had them down cold. My parents didn't suspect a thing.

On Monday afternoon, Shirley gave up a chance to see Debbie Reynolds bat her eyelashes in *Second Time Around* because she wanted to finish the poster she was working on. Shirley had turned the *W*'s in *SNOW WHITE* into two crowns, with the queen's face under one and Snow White under the other. Then she'd taken the *A* in *DWARFS* and made it into a cap on a funny little man.

Shirley's poster was hanging outside Miss Latta's office on Wednesday when Donald, Alan, Joyce, Gloria, and I went to ask her if we could work on the scenery after school. The play was only a week away and the woods needed a few more finishing touches.

"I have a meeting downtown so I'll have to lock that room before I leave," Miss Latta said. Then she must have seen the look on our faces. "I'd love to see what you've done so far, though."

When we all went into the storage room, she stood there and didn't say anything at first. She moved into the middle of the room and turned around slowly. Twice.

I heard her say, "This is incredible." She looked at every animal in the forest. She looked at herself in the mirror. She touched the plates and cups in the china cabinet.

"I feel as if I could take one down and make a cup of coffee. I'm going to call Mr. Chamberlain and invite him here to see this." She turned to where we were standing by the doorway. "You're the children who did this?"

"We did part of it," I said.

She pointed at me and Gloria. "Lift the forest section off the wall and turn it around, will you, please?" The cardboard was hung by ropes so we walked it around and slipped the loops back over the hooks.

"Artists always sign their paintings," Miss Latta explained. "It's an old tradition which shouldn't be broken now. Give me the names of the children who worked on this so I can write them down here on the back."

We named all the kids who weren't there.

"Now I want you to sign your own names," she said.

Joyce stepped forward and wrote her name first. Then Gloria went up, then Donald.

"I don't have a pencil," I said. Alan handed me his. I used it to sign the name that's on my birth certificate. Then I gave it back to him to use.

"I owe you one," he said just loud enough for me to hear when he handed it back to me. "Remember?"

The names were pretty far apart until I wrote mine and Alan wrote his like this:

Julianne Rose Langer
Alan Gianino

Then the boys turned the forest around the right way and we all went home.

It's important not to make too much out of things. I know you shouldn't get confused between what you want to have happen and what really does happen, because you can get in a lot of trouble that way. You can build a castle out of air, and when you go to live in it, it won't be there.

But everything that went on in that room had a magic about it. When Alan and I were in there, it seemed as if we belonged together. Maybe the story of Snow White cast a spell over us. Maybe I cast a spell over myself, but whatever the truth is, it doesn't matter anymore. Whenever I think about what happened that afternoon, I think about it this way.

That that was the afternoon Alan and I carved our names on the back of one of the trees in that forest.

In our forest.

And I had his pencil to prove it.

When I got home, my mother was in the middle of sewing slipcovers and halfway through a quart of peppermint-stick ice cream. I pushed Hope up and down in her bouncing chair. I played peekaboo with her and made her laugh.

"Where did you get these overalls with the heart on them?" I asked my mother when she turned around to watch us.

"Cousin Adele's store," she said.

"Hope looks cute in them."

My mother looked surprised. "You were a very cute baby, too."

56

"Then I got worse."

"No, then you improved. You grew hair."

"Then maybe there's hope for Hope," I said, rubbing the soft peach fuzz on her head.

Frances came over and we put on jackets and went out to sit on my lawn, which looked pretty good since my father had raked the bare spots and picked up all the beer bottles kids had thrown over the picket fence that runs along the sidewalk. As we sat in the cool breeze, I told Frances how much Miss Latta loved the scenery and I promised to show her the place where her name was written.

"It's supposed to be spring, but it's still cold," I said. "Your nose is so red your freckles have disappeared."

"Your face is pale." Frances pushed back her glasses. "You look sick."

"I can't stop shivering."

I began to feel awful, but I figured it was the excitement of holding everything in and not saying anything to my parents. Being too full of happiness can make you feel weak and dizzy. Maybe it was too much for my system to have every dream come true at once.

"I can't believe the weather's this rotten in April." Frances zipped her jacket all the way up and pulled her ponytail out of her collar. "I have to walk the dog when I get home, too, and that stupid animal always thinks I'm taking him out to play. Your teeth are chattering. I bet you have the flu."

"I'm just cold. I better go in." I went across the back

57

porch to the kitchen, and when I got to the door, Frances was still standing in the same spot.

"It better not be serious," she said.

"It's not!" I shouted. Then I went inside and crawled into bed. My mother brought me a glass of ginger ale. She pressed her lips against my forehead.

"You're burning up. I think you have a fever." She unbuttoned my shirt so that I could get into pajamas.

My whole body was covered with spots.

"Chicken pox," said Dr. Kopkind.

He was smiling down at me, but I wasn't smiling back at him, even though I loved his funny face. Only one side of his face could smile. The other half was paralyzed because he'd gotten shot in the war in Korea. His face twisted up when he smiled, but I'd seen that face every time I'd gotten sick since I could remember, and I thought it was one of the nicest faces in the world.

I tried to sit up on the examining table in his office, but I was worn out from the walk, even though it was only three blocks from my house.

"I've got to go to school," I said.

"You've got to stay in bed, young lady. It's nothing serious as long as you take care of yourself."

"I have to go to school!" I grabbed hold of Dr. Kopkind's arm where he had rolled up his sleeve. I was afraid Mrs. McKay would give my part to somebody else. "It's important. I can't miss school!"

"You can go back as soon as the rash disappears." Dr.

Kopkind started stroking my hand and that made every-thing worse. I hate it when people think they're being nice and don't even know they're being awful. My eyes filled up with boiling hot tears.

"Something big going on at school?" he asked my mother.

"Not that I know of."

"I have to get back," I whispered. I was so tired.

"Your mother can call your teacher and tell her you'll be back by the beginning of next week, no problem. If you rest over the weekend, you'll only miss Thursday and Friday. You'll be back at school by Monday. Whatever it is will keep."

"No, it won't." I turned my head toward the wall and cried and cried until the paper on the examining table under my face soaked through.

"Come on, baby," my mother said, pulling a shirt sleeve over one hand. "I'll tell Mrs. McKay you want to go to school, but the doctor won't let you."

I shook my head. There'd be only four days left when I got back and I hadn't rehearsed a single scene with Alan yet.

"Everything will work out, Julie. You'll see."

The minute we got home, I sat down at the kitchen table. Hope was upstairs at my grandmother's. My father wasn't home yet.

"Call her now," I said.

"I'll call as soon as you're in bed."

"I want you to call right now." I was having trouble

holding my head up, so I laid my head in my arms on the table.

"OK," my mother sighed. She got the telephone number from a PTA list. She picked up the phone and talked for a minute. "Mrs. McKay will call back tonight. Let me get you into bed."

I didn't fight. I was so weak, my mother had to help me up into the bed. I took a sip of ginger ale because my mouth was so dry. It felt good to lay my head on a soft pillow and close my eyes. The next thing I knew I heard the phone ring. Then my mother was standing over me and she was smiling down at me the way she used to when I was little.

"Mrs. McKay said not to worry. She said it won't do a bit of harm if you miss the next few days." My mother went on talking for a while, but I didn't hear the rest. I hardly felt the aching in my body, either. I was off in an enchanted forest and a deer with brown eyes and long black horns was watching over me.

CHAPTER TEN

Never Trust an Old Friend

*B*eing sick in bed can be nice. Hope's crib got moved up to my grandmother's apartment because I was contagious, and my mother was doing everything she could to keep Hope from getting sick, too. My mother made me a bed on the couch in the living room, and while she did the bills for Cousin Adele's store, I watched television and read comic books. Even though my mother had to be upstairs with Hope a lot, she promised we could spend fifteen minutes out of every hour together.

My mother found a bag of yarn scraps and taught me how to knit on giant needles. She baked an angel cake and the two of us ate the whole thing for lunch one day. She read me parts of *Alice in Wonderland,* making up funny voices for all the characters, while I leaned my head against her shoulder. Even though my father said it wasn't fair for the woman you married to turn into an obese blimp, she felt good to me, all warm and soft against my cheek.

It was fun being together again. I thought my mother seemed a lot more relaxed with Hope out of the way.

"It isn't easy having a baby when you're thirty-six," she said. "I had a lot more energy when you were little."

"You wanted to have Hope, didn't you?"

"What a question, Julie." That's what my mother always says when she doesn't want to answer. "It's just that it would have been easier if the two of you were a little closer in age. The way it is now, it's like having two separate families. What I need is two of me. Maybe three."

Her face looked funny when she said, "Maybe three." I guess my father wasn't doing so great sharing my mother with Hope, either.

"I liked it better before," I said, feeling close even though she was sitting at the end of the couch by my feet. "I never get to talk to you anymore. I didn't even get to tell you —" But I stopped myself. In less than a week my mother would know all about the play. "I know it's not Hope's fault. It makes me feel bad about myself inside, but sometimes I hate her. I wish she'd never been born." I wiggled my toes, slipping them into a nice warm spot under my mother's legs, but she moved.

"Don't get up," I said. I couldn't see her face. She began stuffing all the balls of yarn back into the bag.

"Time's up," she said, even though there were three minutes left. "Hope's probably awake. I have to go save your grandmother."

"Will you turn the TV back on?" I coughed and a whole lot of phlegm came up in my throat.

62

"Heaven only knows how you picked up a cold in the last few days," my mother grumbled. "Thank God your spots are fading."

I must have fallen asleep after my mother left. She woke me for dinner and tried to get me to eat macaroni, but I wasn't hungry. My father came back from driving my grandmother to Friday night services and talked to me from across the room.

"I don't want to get your germs," he said like a broken record. That's my father's bedside routine when anyone gets sick. Then came the explanation. "I can't afford to miss work or we'll all end up in the poorhouse."

My father's father was burned in a fire when my dad was fifteen. When his father died, my father had to leave school and go to work in a factory to help support the family. He said that being on his own made him tough, but no matter how tough he was, I knew he was still afraid of two things. Being poor and being sick.

"How are you doing?" he asked.

"I'm going back to school on Monday. Dr. Kopkind promised —" I started coughing so bad that I couldn't talk any more. My mother came in and helped me into my room and tucked me into bed. She plugged in the vaporizer. I dozed and listened to the friendly sound of the water bubbling and the steam hissing.

It was dark in my room when I woke up. The water in the vaporizer had boiled away. I was having trouble breathing. It took all my strength to push the covers off and climb out of bed. I could hear my parents' voices in the kitchen, but they sounded far away, too far away to hear me. I took a few steps and then leaned against the wall because my legs wobbled like cooked spaghetti. By the time I got to the kitchen, I had to stand in the doorway to rest. They didn't know I was there.

"Julie's so jealous, it scares me, Hal," my mother was saying. I couldn't believe she was talking about me behind my back, but she was.

"I just don't know what to do, and it's getting worse, not better." I could see her leaning forward over the table, as if she were trying to make my father see how bad I was. "Sometimes I think I should ask her to baby-sit for Hope, but I'm not sure I can trust her."

How could she say that when it wasn't true? All of a sudden, I couldn't breathe at all. I tried to suck air into my lungs, but it made a whooping noise. Then I started choking. My father looked up and saw me, but my mother's voice just went on saying terrible things about me.

I wanted my mother so much. I tried to call her, but something hit me right over the eye and the pain stopped me from saying anything at all.

Later my father said he jumped out of his chair to try and catch me, but he was too late. I had already hit the floor.

Dr. Kopkind came to the house. I looked up and there he was. I was in my parents' four-poster bed and the vaporizer was hissing again, only this time it sounded scary and mean.

"My spots are gone," I said. Then I looked at my mother

64

and a sick feeling filled up my stomach when I remembered what she'd said about me.

"First I'm going to warm this up," said Dr. Kopkind, breathing on his stethoscope. "I want to listen to those pretty lungs of yours." He pressed the stethoscope against my chest and then slipped it against my back. He took my temperature. He sat down on the bed and held my hand.

"You're a pretty sick girl," he said, "so we are going to take very good care of you." He got up. "Sounds like double pneumonia," he told my mother. He went into the kitchen. I could hear him dialing the telephone and I knew something terrible was going to happen.

"He promised I could go back to school on Monday."

"We're going to bring you to the hospital," my mother said. My father was far away, standing in the doorway, trying not to get my germs.

"No, I won't go. I won't let you send me to the hospital."

"Sweetheart, listen," my mother said.

"I'm not going. I can't. I need to go to school."

My mother had my shoes in her hand. She reached under the covers and pulled out one leg. Dr. Kopkind came back.

"They'll be waiting for her," he said.

"No! No! No!" I started screaming at the top of my lungs. Then my voice broke in half. My mother stuck a shoe on my left foot.

"I'll be good. I promise," I croaked to Dr. Kopkind. I grabbed hold of his hand. "Please don't send me away. I'll do anything you want."

"The hospital's the only place we can really take care of you, Julie." He put his arms around me and lifted me into a sitting position. "I'm asking you to trust an old friend. It's just for a few days. I promise you it's going to be all right."

My mother had both my shoes on. I pulled myself out of Dr. Kopkind's arms and crawled over the blankets. I grabbed hold of one of the posts at the bottom of the bed and wrapped myself around it.

"Let me stay home," I begged. "I'm sorry about Hope. I'll never say anything bad about her again."

I searched their faces, looking for just one person to stand up for me. My mother and father were smiling at me, but it was the kind of smile you see in a nightmare when something bad is coming to get you. My parents were smiling so that I wouldn't be afraid, but I could see in their eyes that they were going to do whatever they wanted and I couldn't stop them.

"I'll carry her," said my father. He came into the room walking fast, as if he were in a hurry to get in and out. He threw a blanket around me and lifted my body into his arms. He swung me off the bed, but my hands were still holding tight to the carved pineapple at the top of the post.

My mother started crying, "Julie, please! Hal, stop it!" Then she let out a gasp because all that was left of the bedpost was a sharp white spike full of twisted splinters where the pineapple had broken off in my hands.

66

CHAPTER ELEVEN

Lesson for the Day

My father carried me out to the car. His body was stiff from trying to hold me so far away from him that I couldn't get my arms around his neck. He put me in the front seat, then went around and climbed in behind the wheel. My mother pushed in beside me.

"Hon, your going to the hospital has nothing to do with Hope —" she started, but I pulled the blanket up over my head so that I wouldn't have to look at either of them, and after that, her words were nothing but a bunch of sounds. When we got to the hospital, my father carried me until he found a wheelchair in the lobby. He dropped me into it. Then he hurried out to find a parking space. My mother wheeled me up to the main desk and stood there answering questions:

Name?

Age?

Insurance number?

Someone will be down to bring her to the ward in a minute.

No, you don't need to go with her, Mrs. Langer. Our staff is trained to deal with children entering the hospital. Besides, the other children on the ward are sleeping and your presence will only make it harder for her when it's time for you to leave.

She's a big girl. I don't think you need to worry.

Ah, here's the attendant now. Does Julie have an overnight bag? Good. Then she's all set.

It's better if you go now.

I sat in the wheelchair, curled up under the blanket, and I didn't ask my mother to come up to the children's ward with me. I didn't ask if we could wait for my father to come back from parking the car so I could say good-bye to him. I didn't even make my mouth into a kiss when my mother kissed me and said, "I'll be back to see you tomorrow."

I didn't look at any of the other children when they wheeled me to a bed on the ward. I didn't answer the nurse when she asked me, "Are you comfortable? Do you want anything?" I didn't make a sound when a nurse came in later, pulled down the sheet, and gave me a wicked shot in the behind.

I closed my eyes, but I didn't sleep.

I wished I were dead, but I didn't cry.

I knew I'd never get to be Snow White or dance a waltz with Alan, but I didn't care because now I knew how Snow

68

White must have felt, lying in her coffin with a piece of apple stuck in her throat.

Scared, and empty, and too sad to move.

Mrs. McKay said that fairy tales teach you lessons about real life and this is what I learned: sometimes you can be alive and still feel dead.

CHAPTER TWELVE

Visiting Time

"See, the hospital isn't that bad," my mother told me the next morning. After all, she said, they let me sip water out of a straw that bent in half so I could drink lying down, and there was a way to crank up the bed so that my head went up and my feet went down. They brought me a menu every morning and let me pick out what I wanted to eat. She didn't know that all the food looked like mashed potatoes in different colors, even the desserts.

Before the nurses gave a shot, they'd rub hard with alcohol and say, "Just relax. This will only hurt for a second," but I was too scared to relax so it hurt longer, and then there were four hours of waiting for the next shot. Time passed so slowly, it hardly seemed to move at all.

The place was full of fake smiles. "Now swallow this, dearie!" "Have you been to the bathroom, honey?" "Just relax, sweetie. This will only hurt for a second." I guess people tried to be friendly.

Not everyone, though. I didn't.

I was good, so good they told my mother I was one of the best patients on the ward. I smiled when I didn't feel like smiling. I ate when I didn't feel like swallowing. I never caused the nurses any trouble, but I didn't feel like talking, not even to Dr. Kopkind when he stopped by every morning to tell me how much I was improving.

I didn't ask when they were going to let me go home. I didn't read, or go down the hall to the room where they had toys and games. I was careful never to ask what time it was. That way I didn't worry about whether my mother would be late for visiting hours. For most of that first weekend, all I did was sleep.

On Monday my mother brought me a kitten jigsaw puzzle from Cousin Adele and three Archie comic books from Frances, Gloria, and Shirley. On Tuesday night, she stopped by for only a few minutes because she had to go help my grandmother Rachael with some of the cooking for Passover. When she came to see me on Wednesday, she was carrying a big yellow envelope full of letters the kids had written me from school.

"Where's Daddy?" I asked her.

"He'd like to come, but he's got pneumonia, too. They call it walking pneumonia, whatever that is. The doctor wanted to put your father in the hospital, but he refused. He's afraid he'll die if he ever sets foot in one of these places. He gets a shot from some doctor near his office and then he goes to work. Of course, he's not planning to go to Passover at my mother's." Her mouth twisted at the corners. "I don't know why I keep thinking one of these days he'll change."

"Will you tell him I hope he feels better?"

"Silly, he knows. Your grandmother Hessie wishes she could come too, but everyone agrees it's too much of a risk for her to come to a hospital ward at her age. She misses you." My mother pulled the curtains closed around my bed and sat in the chair. "Let me raise the mattress, Julie. I have to talk to you." She turned the crank handle until our heads were on the same level.

"When I went over to pick up these letters, Mrs. McKay told me you were going to be in the class play tomorrow night. It was very embarrassing to have to tell her I didn't know a thing about it."

"I was going to tell you, but then I decided to keep it a surprise."

"Now I can see why you were so upset about getting sick. I'm so sorry, Julie, but how can you expect me to understand if you don't tell me what's going on?"

I remembered how she acted after I told her how I felt about Hope, but I wanted to be good, so I didn't say anything about that. I started to get excited now that I was finally getting the chance to tell her about the play.

"Did Mrs. McKay tell you I got picked to be Snow White?"

"She did, hon. That's a very big honor."

"At first, I wasn't even going to try out. I thought it was hopeless, but Mrs. McKay asked *me* to try out. Did you see the scenery we made?"

"No."

"We had to make a forest and a cottage and the queen's mirror. We wanted it to be perfect because this is the first play the sixth grade ever put on. It might be the first play some of the littler kids ever see."

"That's why I was so surprised when Mrs. McKay told me she had picked that particular play. I wished you had told me. I would have liked to have said something."

"About what?"

"About choosing a play like *Snow White* in a school that is racially mixed."

"What?" I stared at my mother as if her face could explain what she was talking about. It looked the way it did when my mother was trying to be nice.

"Darling, this may be hard to understand, but it's just as well that you're not going to be in that play tomorrow. I know you're disappointed, but I think the school is making a mistake and I don't want our family to be part of it."

"What mistake?"

"*Snow White*'s just not a good play to pick, honey." My mother leaned forward and brushed the hair back from my forehead as if she still loved me. "Especially now, Julie. More than three thousand people have been arrested at 'sit-ins' down south because they were fighting for the right of a black person to sit down at a public lunch counter and order a hamburger just like anyone else."

73

"*Snow White*'s a fairy tale," I said. "Don't you know the story?"

"Darling, think about the words, *snow white*. Snow White stands for everything that's good and pure. How do you think you would feel about that if you didn't have white skin?"

"Nobody at school took it that way." I could feel myself beginning to get upset. "Miss Latta and Mrs. McKay would never do anything like that. You know they wouldn't. All the kids liked the play."

"That's the way it felt to you, Julie. You had the lead. Put yourself in Gloria's place."

"Gloria got to be the narrator," I cried out louder than I meant to. "She gets to tell everybody the history of fairy tales. She could have been Snow White, but she didn't want to be Snow White. Why do you always make everybody seem so bad?" I felt as afraid of my mother's thoughts as my father was of my germs.

"I seem to hurt people whether I mean to or not," my mother said. I knew she was thinking about what she'd said about me to my father the night I went to the hospital. "I'm not saying anybody did it on purpose!"

We must have been talking loudly enough for the nurse to hear, because she pushed back the curtain and asked, "Is everything all right, Mrs. Langer?" My mother answered in a voice that meant that she was tired of having everything go wrong and wanted to get away.

"No, I've gotten Julie upset about something by choosing the wrong time to bring it up and everything I say seems to be making it worse. I'm exhausted. This has been a very difficult week for me. I was supposed to be home an hour ago. Can you stay with her until she quiets down?"

I heard her chair scraping on the floor. I heard my mother pick up her pocketbook and drop the envelope filled with letters on the metal shelf that went across my bed.

I wanted to say, "Don't go home."

I wanted to say, "I'm sorry. I know you didn't mean to get me upset."

I wanted to say, "I waited for you all day because I missed you so much."

But I didn't say any of those things. I just buried my face in the thick hospital pillows and listened to my mother's footsteps going down the ward and into the hall, going home and leaving me behind.

CHAPTER THIRTEEN

Messages from School

*W*hen supper came, all I ate was tapioca pudding. After the nurse took the tray away, I opened the yellow envelope. It was filled with letters on notebook paper.

First I read what Frances wrote:

Dear Julie,

I talked to your mother and she said your O.K. so I don't have to wish you get well soon, no matter what Mrs. M said. (Just kidding!) GET WELL SOON!!!

Joyce is Snow White. Mrs. M asked her to learn your lines while you were out with chicken pocks "just in case." Joyce acts like she wanted to be Snow White all the time.

You'll never guess what else. Gloria is the queen. She didn't want to do it at first, but she changed her mind when Mrs. M told her that Christopher would be her servent. Gloria even got extra lines. "Hunter, you must obey me. My wish is your command."

The only reason Christopher didn't quit is he gets to drag her out of Snow White's wedding. He told Donald that the night of the play he's going to knock Gloria on the floor and drag her off by the legs. Everybody thinks he's just shooting off his mouth, tho.

Also, Gloria is going to wear beaded earrings her mother says come from Africa. Mrs. G. told Gloria she can be a black queen just like the queen of Sheba. Gloria is out of her mind with happiness.

I saved the best news for last. Guess who gets to be the narrater? ME. I get to read what Gloria wrote about fairy tales and my mother promised to get me new glasses and a pair of patent leather heels with pointy toes. I already picked them out.

> Don't let the bedbugs get you.
> Your friend,
> Frances

Shirley's was short:

Dear Julie,

Remember when I was just a lady in waiting. I still am but now I am make-up man, too. I collected a bunch of stuff from everybodys mother. I am trying it out on kids after school and I am learning a lot

of tricks. If your home, we can get together over
Easter vacation. Did you get the comick books?

                              Wish you could still be in it.
                                            Love,
                                              Shirley

Joyce's was even shorter:

Dear Julie,

It's terrible that you got sick and can't be in the
play. I hope they let you come home from the
hospital.

                              Sincerely,
                                Your friend,
                                  Joyce

But it was Gloria's letter that really got to me:

Dear Julie,

I'm really excited about getting to play the queen
except for that fact that I don't get to strangle Joyce.
Alan doesn't even come on stage until Joyce is practically dead, but that doesn't stop Joyce from making
a play for him. Mrs. McKay had to tell her that she
shouldn't have one hand beside her head and the
other hanging over the side like she was in bed instead of a corps in a coffin.

When Alan stands over her saying, "Who is this
beautiful maiden?" she's supposed to keep her eyes

closed, but she looks right up at him. All the kids think they should put a sheet over her face. Mrs. McKay showed them how to waltz and Diane told me that Joyce and Alan are practicing after school at her house, and her mother isn't home either.

When we brought the funny books over to your mother, she said you were feeling better. I hope so, because if you don't get back to school quick, Alan and Joyce will be as good as married (if you know what I mean). If Mrs. McKay doesn't watch out, this play will be too dirty for little kids to see.

I wish they would let you out of the hospital in time to see it. My costume is gorgous.

Get well soon,
Gloria

I looked through the rest of the letters. Nick wrote:

Too bad you got sick. The play stinks now.

Christopher's note read:

It is rotten you didnt get to be snow white you worked hard and now you are missing the best part. Dont let them docters near your liver. P.S. I got a real hunting nife. Ill show you when you get back.

Most of the letters said "Get well soon," and stuff like that. I read every one. I went through them again to make sure that two of them hadn't got stuck together. Then I put my hand all the way down into the yellow envelope to make sure there wasn't one in there.

Then I had to believe it.

Alan was the only one who hadn't written.

CHAPTER FOURTEEN

Back to Reality

My mother brought me home from the hospital on Saturday. I felt so mixed up inside that I couldn't decide whether I was glad or sorry that I hadn't gotten to see the play on Thursday night. I didn't even call Frances to find out how it had gone because staying in the hospital for a whole week made me tired instead of getting me rested, and all I wanted to do when I got home was climb into bed. Just making it up the walk and across the back porch wore me out.

My father carried my stuff into the house, and while my mother was tucking me in, he came and sat on my bed. I guess he figured I wasn't contagious anymore. He'd been working in the yard so his face was tanned, but I could see dark circles under his eyes.

"Are you still sick?" I asked him. "I was worried about you."

"You shouldn't worry about me. I made up my mind not to be sick, and that was that. Sickness is all in the mind anyway. I taught that doctor a thing or two. He probably learned more from treating me than he did in four years of medical school."

"He told me he couldn't wait to see you walk up to your grave and jump in," my mother remarked. I thought that was pretty funny, but my father likes his own jokes best.

"If you want to stay well from here on, Julie, you've got to develop good eating habits. We should start by getting rid of all the sweets in this house. Did you hear that, Eleanor?"

"If sickness is all in the mind, you can eat whatever you want, Julie. See, Hal. I'm listening."

"Your mind is *in* your body. That's why a well-nourished body can take care of itself."

My mother stopped unpacking my clothes. "Well, then, how do you explain the fact that my body, sweets and all, took care of itself while *your* body got pneumonia? I can't wait to hear your wonderful explanation." Hope started howling in the other room. "I'll be back with something to eat, Julie," she said sweetly. "Unfortunately, your father prefers shooting his mouth off to cooking."

After she left, my father started defending himself.

"I've never missed a day of work in my life. Langers are tough as nails."

"Langer girls aren't tough," I answered. "I don't think I'll ever feel like getting out of bed."

82

"Whatever happened to 'I have to get back to school'?"

"I was supposed to be in a play, but it's all over now."

"Your mother told me. Here. I thought it might cheer you up to have something new to wear back to school." My father handed me a brown-paper bag. Inside was a green long-sleeved sweater, the softest wool I'd ever felt. It was the same shade of green as the grass coming up in our yard.

"One hundred percent lamb's wool. It was a sample at one of the mills. I hope it's your size." My father got up to leave, but I didn't want him to go yet.

"It's beautiful," I said quickly. "I missed you when I was in the hospital."

"What's there to miss?" He turned toward me and shrugged his shoulders. "I did you a favor. Who wants to be bothered by a lot of visitors waking them up and making extra work for the nurses? Most people never realize how much better off patients in the hospital would be without them."

"Mummy said you didn't come because hospitals give you the creeps."

My father's eyebrows went up like the tops of two bushy triangles. "Shows how much your mother knows. It happens to be a matter of principle."

I made my face into a cut-out-the-baloney expression so, of course, he had to convince himself he'd convinced me.

"I didn't even go to the hospital to see my own father. In those days, they thought fifteen-year-olds were

83

too young to go up on the wards. Of course, they didn't realize he was dying. I always figured if I missed my father's death, I might as well miss everybody's, including my own. It was one of the smartest decisions I ever made." Sometimes I thought my father actually believed himself.

"I wasn't dying."

"You probably would have if I'd come to see you. Try on the sweater." He headed for the door again.

"Did you glue your bed back together?" That stopped him.

"Your mother doesn't agree, of course," he said, standing at the bottom of my bed, "but I like the bed much better the way it is. I hang my shorts on that bedpost every night, and I've always worried that if there was a fire, they'd get stuck on that pineapple. I had nightmares of running outside in the nude. I sleep much better now that I know I can grab them and put them on without a hitch, thanks to you."

My father is such a nut, he made me smile.

"See, the world didn't come to an end," he said. "Disappointment is one of the best things in the world. You learn you can survive even when things don't turn out the way you want them to."

"Happy endings are just for fairy tales, right?"

"What?" my father asked, but I didn't bother to repeat it. After he left, I slipped the green sweater on over my pajamas and pretended that it was a big hug. I was glad to be home.

CHAPTER FIFTEEN

Note from a Friend

*E*aster vacation seemed to go on forever. I watched TV game shows, played solitaire, and ate a chocolate candy bar every single day. I read a story about how Sophia Loren used to think she was homely, and I knew Shirley would be interested, but I didn't want to see her or any of my friends. I had my mother tell everyone who called that I couldn't have visitors.

I felt weak inside. They'd cleared up my lungs. Now my mind was in trouble. I felt cut off from everybody whose life had gone on while mine had stopped, and I didn't have the energy to start it again. My body could walk, but the rest of me didn't want to stand without an arm around me, holding me up. I would have been happy to get around the way Hope did, with someone lifting me under the armpits and moving me from place to place.

I didn't feel any better by Monday morning. That's

why I got so mad at my mother for making me carry an umbrella to school when it was just drizzling a little.

"Nobody carries umbrellas," I pleaded. "Do you know how stupid I'll look?"

"You're still recovering from double pneumonia, Julie. Don't make it hard for me. If I had the car, you know I'd drive you, but I don't, so you are going to have to carry that umbrella even if I have to call the school and ask them to make sure it's still up when you arrive."

"OK, I'll take it!" I said, and that's why I walked to school with a pink and purple striped umbrella over my head, looking like a jerk.

I walked as slowly as I could. I didn't get to school until the last bell was ringing. I walked up two flights of empty stairs to the third-floor coatroom, hung the umbrella under my raincoat, and went stright to my seat. I didn't get a chance to talk to anybody. To tell the truth, I didn't feel like talking to anybody.

"Time to get back to work," Mrs. McKay said, as if the play were chalk you could just erase off a blackboard. First off, we had a spelling test. I got three words wrong. That meant I'd have to go through spelling exercises all week. In math, I messed up the decimal places when I multiplied, so every one of my answers was wrong. It was only 10:45 and I hated being back at school already.

I looked around. The posters were all down and the picture books were gone from the corner table. I'd been out of school two and a half weeks and every trace of

Snow White had disappeared. Even John Glenn was missing, pushed off the Current Events board by the Shah of Iran's visit to Washington. His wife was grinning and no wonder. She looked as if she were wearing the world's total supply of jewels at one time.

Heads bent over books. No one else seemed to mind the changes. They all seemed perfectly happy to be back at work again. Even though every friend I had in the world was in that room, I felt all alone. I couldn't think of a single thing to be happy about except that the sun had come out.

When we got dismissed after lunch, I followed Frances down the stairs. She was wearing her new shoes, and so she took the stairs one at a time, holding on to the banister.

"Walk around with me," she said, once we got outside. "I need to practice."

"Where are Gloria and Shirley?"

"Miss Latta's writing a report on how much we improved from putting on the play, so she asked some kids to come answer questions during recess. That's where Gloria and Alan are. Shirley's over there."

We'd reached the end of the building, and when we turned, I could see Joyce and Shirley head-to-head by the fence. Joyce was holding up the mirror on her gold compact and Shirley was putting on mascara with a little brush.

"Joyce goes to this modeling school that shows you how to put on makeup and she's teaching Shirley. She's going to bleach out Shirley's mustache. If it works, I think I'm going to ask her if she can help me get rid of my freckles."

We walked by some girls jumping rope and one of them almost knocked Frances over. "You better hold on to me," I said. "How did the play go?"

"Thursday night, the whole room was packed. We had to come out five times at the end because the audience wouldn't stop clapping. When we did it for the younger kids, afterwards they all wanted to come up and touch us."

"That sounds good."

"My mother loved the scenery. It's too bad the janitor already put it all in the basement. Oh, and you would have died if you saw Gloria. She screamed so loud at Snow White's wedding, the police probably thought it was a murder. I was pretty good myself. My mother could hear me reading the introduction way back in the last row. Do you think I look normal in these things, or like I'm going to trip?"

"You're getting better."

"My mother says I look like I'm drunk."

"That's because your new glasses are on crooked. How come they're taped at the corner?"

"The dog chewed them. My mother took a fit." Frances let go of me and started wobbling toward the door. "Everybody's mad at you, you know, because you didn't call when you got home from the hospital. Why did you act like such a snob this morning? You didn't look over at me once."

"It's just so boring to be back," I said, catching up to her. "What's the point? There's nothing to look forward to."

"Somebody from the School Department took pictures of the play, and I can't wait to see those." The bell rang. "Besides, Mrs. McKay said we might do something for Memorial Day."

"I'll see you in class. I have to fix my hair." I ducked into the bathroom in the basement. I looked at my hair, which curled under on one side and stuck out on the other. I looked tired and awful and I knew I could never explain why I didn't call anyone when I got back from the hospital. I felt so angry, angry, angry—about missing the best two weeks of school, about how everybody just loved Joyce all of a sudden, about how I never got to have a happy ending in my life, even though it wasn't my fault I got sick. If I hadn't been wearing my new green sweater, I would have gone home, but I couldn't let my father down. He wouldn't have run away if every kid in the school hated him.

I walked into class late. I guess Mrs. McKay didn't say anything because she knew I'd been sick. I'd left my math book on my desk and there was a piece of paper sticking out from under it. I sat down, and after Mrs. McKay handed out maps so we could start marking down the names of the oceans and continents, I lifted up the book and read the note.

I looked around. Alan was watching Mrs. McKay at the board. Shirley was peeking at her face in a little mirror. Gloria was writing something on her map, and Joyce was sharpening her pencil. Frances leaned forward and whispered, "What does it say?"

"Nothing," I answered.

I folded the note and slipped it into my desk. I didn't need to see it to remember nine words:

ALAN SAID HE WISHED
YOU DROPPED DEAD.
A FRIEND

CHAPTER SIXTEEN

Revenge

*T*he rest of the day went by in a blur. I didn't want everybody watching me to see how I was taking the news, so I kept my face buried in my books. No one was going to have the fun of seeing me burst into tears.

When it was time to go home, we had to get our coats and bring them back to our seats. The last thing I wanted to do was to carry that stupid umbrella in front of every kid in that class. Going out to the coatroom, I kept my eyes looking down at my feet, but coming back, I had to walk up the outside aisle past Alan. I made myself look right at him. I didn't want to give him the satisfaction of thinking I couldn't face him.

He noticed my umbrella. Then he turned and whispered something to Walter, who sat in the seat behind him. He put his hand up in front of his mouth so that I couldn't tell what he was saying. He and Walter started laughing as if I were a big joke.

I glared at Alan, my coldest full-of-hate look, and he stopped snickering. His mouth curled up at the edges, and I saw on his face the same fake smile my parents had worn the night they sent me to the hospital. It's like a mask people use to cover up their true feelings, but if you look in their eyes, you can see they're not listening to you, that they're not even trying to understand you, that they really don't care.

Alan grinned up at me and it was as if he enjoyed making fun of everything that had happened to me. It was a smart-aleck grin. It was a show-off grin, and I wanted to wipe it right off his stupid face if it was the last thing I ever did.

As I came up to him, I lifted up my umbrella. Alan stopped smiling all right, and his mouth opened up into a little *O* before he brought his arm up in front of his face and tried to twist away. I brought the umbrella down with all my might and I hit him so hard that he fell out of his seat onto the floor without making a sound. The next thing I knew Joyce was screaming. Then Mrs. McKay was bending over Alan's body so that I couldn't see how badly he was hurt.

"Go to the office and wait for me there," Mrs. McKay ordered, without looking up. I just stood there.

"Julie," she hissed. "Go to the office this minute!"

I dropped the umbrella and it fell on the floor, all bent in the middle with one spoke sticking out. Then I turned and ran out of the room.

CHAPTER SEVENTEEN

Facing the Consequences

I walked down one flight of stairs and stopped in front of Miss Latta's door. The bench against the wall was empty, but I didn't want to sit where everyone could stare at me on the way out. The storage room where we'd worked on the scenery wasn't locked, so I pushed the door open and looked in. It was filled with buckets and brooms, boxes of soap powder and baskets of trash. It looked as if someone had used our woods for a garbage dump.

I heard kids leaving their classrooms so I slipped inside. I could hear shouting as everyone rushed out of the building. Then I heard someone knocking on Miss Latta's door. She called out, "Who is it?" Mrs. McKay answered, "Carol," and went in. I closed my eyes and leaned against the wall.

When I was in second grade, Miss Latta used to walk around the schoolyard every recess. All the girls wanted to walk with her and hold her hand. I always used to try and squeeze in next to her. One recess, she picked me to go and find out the time. I looked at the clock in the first-grade room and I couldn't make any sense of it. I guess no one had taught me how to tell time. I hid in the girls' room until the bell rang, and even though Miss Latta never said a word to me about it, I couldn't face her for a long time after that.

Remembering that made me laugh. Here I was, hiding from her again. Only this time I didn't ever want to come out.

I heard voices in the hall. Then the storeroom door creaked on its hinges. When I opened my eyes, there was a streak of light from the open door right at my feet.

"Julie?" Miss Latta asked softly.

I took one step forward into the brightness.

"Julie, what happened?"

"I hit Alan Gianino with my umbrella."

"Julie, I've known you since you entered school and you never hit anyone in your whole life. Come over here." Her shadow on the floor reached out a hand, but I couldn't move.

"How are you feeling? I know you've been very sick."

I didn't want anybody feeling sorry for me, so I told her again, "I knocked him on the floor."

"What did Alan do to deserve that?"

"Nothing."

"Then why did you hit him?"

Miss Latta's shadow came closer and then I felt her arm around my shoulders. I closed my eyes so tears wouldn't leak out and we walked across the hall into her office. We went over to the corner she used as a little library and she made me sit down in the soft chair next to her bookshelves. She handed me a box of tissues and her silver circle earrings fluttered back and forth under her pageboy. Then she sat down at her desk and didn't say a word.

"Is Alan all right?" I asked.

"You're the one I'm worried about. You must be very upset."

"I knocked him out." I said each word very clearly, as if she were deaf. "I left him dead cold on the floor."

"As soon as you left, he got up again. He wasn't physically hurt, though there are other ways people can be hurt, you know."

When she said the word *hurt,* I felt it all over again, how much I wanted somebody else to hurt for once, somebody else to pay for things being so unfair. "Serves him right," I said under my breath. Miss Latta heard me.

"He must have really hurt you."

"You wouldn't understand." She didn't say anything to that so there was a long silence.

"When Mrs. McKay got your books together, Julie, she found this." Miss Latta took the note from on top of some books on her desk and handed it to me. I stared at the words until they got all blurred. I grabbed some tissues and pressed them against my eyes.

"I didn't get to be Snow White, right?" I said. "I didn't get to be in the play at all. I got left out of everything. Wasn't that enough for him?"

"What Alan thinks matters to you, doesn't it?"

"Not anymore." I felt tough when I said that, tough as nails.

"Well, you matter to him."

I took the tissues away. I didn't want her to lie to me. "He doesn't care about me."

"Julie, listen. When a boy chases a girl and takes her scarf, why is he teasing her? It's because he likes her and doesn't know a better way to show it yet."

"This isn't anything like taking a scarf."

"You were sick and Alan obviously felt something about it." Miss Latta pointed to the note. "This is how it came out. It may be hard to understand, Julie, but sometimes people can be so afraid of something happening that they wish it would happen just so they can stop being afraid."

"What did *he* have to be afraid of?"

"It's only a guess, but I suspect Alan might have been worried that what happened to his mother might happen to you."

"I don't believe that."

"Well, whatever he was feeling, it doesn't excuse his remark, just as your feelings are no excuse for hitting him." I nodded because I agreed with her. "All of us have times when we'd like to solve our problems by striking out, but growing up means learning how to express feelings with words and *not* with actions. The rule in this school is two weeks of detention for hitting another child and I can't make any exceptions. You'll have to come down here after school, starting tomorrow. And I want to talk to your mother."

"I'll tell her." I put the note back on her desk and gathered up my books. When Miss Latta opened the door, Frances and Gloria were waiting for me in the hall. For a minute, no one said anything, but I guess Miss Latta was still curious about the note. She had to know everything that was going on in the whole school.

"Does either one of you know who left that note on Julie's desk?"

"It wasn't Frances or me," said Gloria, "and Joyce was with Shirley all through recess."

"Frances? Gloria? Did you hear Alan say he wished Julie would drop dead?"

Frances looked upset and surprised. "Is that what the note said?" I wished Miss Latta would drop the whole subject, but she wouldn't leave it alone.

"Did you hear him say it, Frances?"

"Not exactly."

"But you knew he'd said it?"

"Everyone was teasing Alan," Gloria interrupted. "He'd be doing a scene with Joyce, and kids would say, 'Wait till your girl friend finds out,' or 'Is that how you do it with Julie?' Stuff like that."

"And he got angry?"

"It was all Nick's fault," Frances burst out. "He was the worst. Nick kept saying Alan should go to the hospital because one kiss from Alan would fix her up."

Miss Latta slipped her hands into the pockets of her gray skirt. We all watched her thinking.

"I'm not sure that what people say when they're being teased should be held against them," she said finally. "Everyone does things and says things under pressure, and then it's too late to take it back. Most of us count on the fact that people who care about us will forgive and forget. I want you to think about that, anyway."

I thought everything was settled, but Miss Latta went back into her office with a puzzled look still on her face. Then the three of us were alone.

"Two weeks' detention," I said.

"Shirley wanted to wait with us," said Frances, "but there's a TV special for women about 'The Glamour Trap,' and she didn't want to miss it."

"Let's get out of here!" Gloria grabbed our hands and pulled Frances and me toward the stairs. "If I ever find the kid who wrote that note, I'm going to kill 'em."

"Gloria!" Frances stopped so she wouldn't lose her balance on her new shoes. "Didn't you hear what Miss Latta said? Forgive and forget."

"I'd rather die," I said.

"Nope. Frances is right," Gloria said. "We shouldn't kill 'em. I'll hold 'em so you can beat 'em over the head with your umbrella." She let out a giant cackle, and even Frances smiled in spite of herself.

All of a sudden, I had the feeling everything was going to work out all right.

Alan could go to hell.

CHAPTER EIGHTEEN

A Full Confession

By the time I got home, that scary feeling of being all alone was gone. My friends were my friends again. My father had given me a beautiful new sweater. And that disgusting umbrella was probably in the trash. I still had to explain to my mother why I'd gotten two weeks' detention, but I didn't think she'd be that mad when she found out the whole story.

I walked into the kitchen and there was Cousin Adele sitting at the table wearing a black dress with a bright yellow jacket. She had on nylons and high-heeled shoes, and her hair was sprayed so that it looked as if it belonged on a department-store dummy. There were two baskets of laundry in the middle of the kitchen floor. The breakfast dishes were still on the table, along with a half-empty box of brownies. Hope was sitting on my mother's lap, smearing applesauce everywhere. From the way Cousin Adele was sitting, I could tell she was hoping none of the mess would rub off on her.

The minute I saw her, my heart sank.

"Eleanor, doesn't the girl own a comb?" Cousin Adele asked. "How can you let her go out looking like that?"

I waited for my mother to defend me the way she sticks up for my father, but she didn't say one word. All of a sudden she was busy checking Hope's diaper.

"I've been sick," I said.

"Well, I know that, but a little bit of rouge would make all the difference in the world. You're so pale to begin with. And that haircut . . ." Cousin Adele shook her head and her hair moved with it like a block of cement.

"Don't you want to thank Adele for her gift?" my mother hinted.

"Thanks for the puzzle," I said, forcing out the words. It's hard to be grateful to a skinflint who always buys her presents in her own store.

"I stopped by the hospital to see you, dear, but by the time we closed up shop, you were sleeping. Did the nurses tell you I'd come by?"

"Umm," I mumbled, taking off my coat.

"That's a gorgeous sweater," Cousin Adele commented. "I bet it's a lot nicer than what the other girls in that school are wearing. She must stick out like a sore thumb, El."

I thought my mother was going to say something at last, but she reached for a brownie instead.

"This sweater was a gift from a very generous person.

My father," I said. "I have to go up and see my grand-mother."

I ran upstairs without waiting for permission and stayed in my grandmother's apartment, watching out the window for Cousin Adele's shiny black Buick to drive away. When I came down, Hope was chewing on a plastic ring. My mother was cleaning up the kitchen.

"How was your first day back at school?" my mother asked.

"All right, except that someone left a note on my desk. It said that Alan Gianino wished I dropped dead when I was in the hospital."

My mother turned off the water. "Julie, that's just a mean story somebody made up. No one would say a thing like that."

"Frances and Gloria heard him."

"And they told you? What kind of friends are they?"

"They weren't going to say anything, but I got so up-set . . ."

"Of course, you were upset." My mother walked over and started scrubbing the top of the kitchen table. "That's terrible. Awful. And on your first day back, after you've been so sick. I'm going to go talk to Mrs. McKay."

"Miss Latta asked if you'd come in."

"Good. I'd like to find out what child would write that kind of note."

"Nobody knows who did it."

My mother took a swipe at the top of Hope's high-chair

tray and came back to where I was standing by the sink. She put a wet hand on my shoulder.

"Oh, Julie. Kids your age are terribly mean and there's not a thing anyone can do about it. I remember when Adele was about your age. Some boy said she had a face like a rat, and Adele's friend Natalie couldn't wait to repeat it to her. My cousin locked herself in her room for two days. Her brother was going to beat the boy up until he discovered the boy was a foot taller than he was."

"Did anyone ever say anything mean about you?"

"Well, you know how large I am on top. I developed before any of the other girls, and I've always been self-conscious about it. One day, when I was walking home from school, I heard a boy say, 'Here comes the cow.' "

"What did you do?"

"What do you think I did? I cried. When I got home, I put on my mother's girdle and pulled it up across my chest. I wanted to squash myself flat."

"Know what I did?"

My mother put down the dishrag and wiped both hands on her housedress. She looked right at me. "I'm ready. What did you do?"

"I hit him over the head with the umbrella."

"You did not."

"Yes, I did."

"Did you hurt him?"

"He's OK. The umbrella's broken."

"Good riddance to the umbrella. It was one of Cousin Adele's mistakes, but really, that's . . . I mean . . ." My mother reached up with one hand and began rubbing the back of her neck. "Julie, I don't know what to say."

"I got two weeks' detention."

"Which you deserve."

"I know."

"So that's what Miss Latta wants to talk to me about, not about the note, but about my daughter's behavior?"

"You could talk about the note, too."

My mother took a deep breath. She turned around and started washing dishes. "I intend to tell Miss Latta that you have promised never to do a thing like that again." A soapy plate thunked in the drainer.

"I promise."

"I'm not going to say a word about this to your father and I don't want you to tell him. He'll be on the phone for days, bragging about his little spitfire."

"I won't say anything."

"But *I* am not proud of you, Julie. I don't think it shows spunk or spirit to turn on somebody when you're angry and let them have it. I don't admire that." A handful of silverware clattered against the plates.

I knew why my mother was throwing the dishes around, and why she was standing so that I couldn't see her face.

My mother wasn't angry, no matter what she said.

She was smiling.

CHAPTER NINETEEN

Remember to Act Surprised!

Gloria, Shirley, and Frances walked me to school in the morning. I was hoping the kids at school would leave me alone, but my friends were expecting trouble. As it turned out, trouble was waiting for us.

The minute we walked into the schoolyard, Christopher came running toward us with a bunch of boys right behind him.

"You tell me if I ever say anything to make you mad," Christopher yelled at me. "You just tell me, Julie, and I promise I'll take it back before you bean me." The kids behind him started laughing.

"You're makin' her mad now," Gloria warned him.

"She ain't got her umbrella now." Christopher put his palms together. "Would you believe I prayed last night? I prayed for the sun to shine so Julie wouldn't bring no weapons to school."

"You think you're so smart!" Shirley stepped out in front of me. "Why don't you pick on someone your own size?"

Christopher put his hands on his hips. "What you gonna do about it?" he mimicked. Shirley stepped backward right onto my foot.

"It's not worth doing anything about it," Gloria said, "because if we knocked all your brains out nobody would notice the difference anyway."

"I'm so scared," Christopher teased. He was putting on a big show for the crowd now, lapping up all the attention. Until Nick walked up to him.

"You say one more word to Julie, I'm gonna punch you right in the mouth." Nick faced Christopher, fists clenched.

"Can't you take a joke?" Christopher asked. Next to Nick, who's as thick as a tree trunk, Christopher looked like a string bean. He was looking around, trying to think of his next move, when he caught sight of something happening behind me. I could see Christopher's confidence oozing back.

"It's Alan," Frances whispered as a boy pushed past me. He had his jacket hood up so I couldn't see his face. Most kids backed out of the way, but Christopher went right up to Alan and threw an arm around his shoulders.

"Here's my good man," Christopher announced, "back in the ring without a mark on him. That's the thing about getting into a fight with a girl . . ." He walked off, keeping Alan between him and Nick. "It's about the same as being attacked by Bugs Bunny." Alan never even turned around.

"Nick sure sticks up for you," said Frances, as the bell rang. All I could think about was getting a good look at Alan so I could check him out, but instead of getting into reading groups, we had nature study. A man from the Natural History Museum brought in a toad and a frog. Mrs. McKay passed the animals around in a small glass terrarium while Mr. Colby told us all about webbed feet and tongues that hook in the front. Then we saw a movie about amphibians.

By the time we got dismissed for recess, everybody wanted to stretch. Mrs. McKay yelled, "Walk, don't run," while we all piled down the stairs. When we got to the bottom, there were all the photographs from the play tacked to the first-floor bulletin board.

"Oh, my God, look at me!" Gloria pulled me over to a picture of her standing in front of the mirror in a long cape.

"Alan, come over here. You've got to see this," a girl called out. I knew without looking it was Joyce. Alan pushed in next to her. They were practically glued together, looking at a picture of the two of them dancing. Joyce's voice floated over everybody else's. "Don't we look terrific? Isn't this one fabulous?" Alan seemed to love every word.

After everyone else had gone, Frances, Gloria, and Shirley began filling me in on every bit of the play I had missed, picture by picture.

"See the putty Shirley stuck on my nose." Gloria pointed to her face peeking through the cottage window.

"Nobody else could have played that part as good as you," Christopher said, coming up behind us. Gloria turned around and I could see she was pleased. For a minute, we both thought Christopher was trying to make up for the scene he'd started before school.

"You were good, too. There he is, Julie." Gloria pointed to a picture of Christopher standing in the woods, holding a long, wicked-looking knife.

"There's just one thing I don't get," Christopher said, edging toward the door to the schoolyard. "How come you never took off your makeup?" and he ducked outside.

"I'm going to get him," said Gloria.

"Maybe he likes you and he can't think of any other way to show it," I suggested.

"Too bad for him. He's going to be sorry. You wait and see." I could tell Gloria had been a great queen. The way she said it made chills run up and down my neck.

When we got back to class, Mrs. McKay announced we were going to have penmanship. There was a lot of groaning. We hadn't had penmanship since fourth grade.

"Pass back this paper, make sure your pencil is sharp, and write this sentence three times, once in small letters, once entirely in capital letters, and then I'd like to see it in careful, readable handwriting." And she wrote on the board: "Johnny Appleseed wished to make this a bountiful country." I was just finishing when she announced that she wanted to hang them all up.

"Is anyone willing to stay after school and help me?"

"I will," Gloria offered before Mrs. McKay even finished her sentence. I was surprised because Gloria had basketball practice after school every Tuesday.

We were putting our books away for the day when Nick looked out the window and saw my mother coming into the schoolyard. He told Donald, who told Diane, who whispered to Joyce, who passed it on to Frances, who told me. If she'd arrived any later, the school would have been closed, but when I went down after school to sit on the bench, I knew why the door to Miss Latta's office was closed. My mother was inside. In a little while, Mrs. McKay came down the stairs and went inside, too.

There was a book on the bench called *Little Women,* and I sat there reading about four sisters whose father had gone to war and left them poor as church mice. I didn't notice Gloria coming down the stairs until she was right in front of me.

"I took care of Christopher's paper with my little eraser," she whispered. "He's never going to shoot his mouth off again as long as he lives. Just remember to act surprised. I got to get to basketball practice. See you tomorrow." I could hear the school doors slam behind her just as the office door opened. My mother came out, with Miss Latta and Mrs. McKay right behind her.

"We can go upstairs and look right now," Miss Latta was saying. Then she noticed me sitting on the bench. "I hope you enjoy that book, Julie. I left it there because I thought you might. We'll be back in a minute, and then you can go home with your mother." Miss Latta had something in her hand, and when she went past me, she switched it to the other side. In a few minutes, Miss Latta and my mother came back down.

"If every day was like this one, I'd be a nervous wreck," Miss Latta was saying, "but after all these years on the job, nothing surprises me anymore. Don't worry about it, Eleanor. Take your little girl and go home. Thanks for coming in."

"Miss Latta is a wonderful person," my mother said as we walked the two blocks to our house. "She thinks you've had a tough year, doodle." I looked up. My mother hadn't called me that in a long, long time. "New baby sister, missing out on the play, being sick, coming to the end of elementary school — that's a lot to happen in one year. You're growing up fast, do you know that?"

"I'm up to your shoulder." I matched my steps with hers.

"Well, I think it's about time we gave you a little more responsibility. I'm going shopping with Adele on Friday. Will you baby-sit for me?"

"Sure."

"You think you can do it?"

"I know what to do."

"OK. You know I've been worrying about you. I even thought we ought to go see someone at the Guidance Clinic, but after seeing some of the problems Miss Latta has to deal with, I think I can relax."

"What problems?"

"Like Christopher James."

"What did he do?"

"Well, everyone else in the class managed to write 'Johnny Appleseed wished to make this a bountiful country.' Christopher didn't."

"What did he write?"

"I just can't understand what gets into a boy like that."

"Like what?"

"Well, everyone in school is going to know by tomorrow, so there's no reason I shouldn't repeat it, but don't say I told you, will you?" She dropped her voice. "I can't imagine why, but he wrote, 'Johnny Appleseed *pissed* to make this a bountiful country.' Three times."

CHAPTER TWENTY

Alan's Waiting

Christopher's paper was such a mess to begin with that Mrs. McKay wouldn't believe anyone had changed it. "Call the priest," Christopher said, when Mrs. McKay called him up to her desk. "Get me a Bible if you think I'm lying." He held one hand up in the air and pressed the other against his chest. "I swear to God on this cross which was given to me by my uncle who is dead," he vowed, but Mrs. McKay ignored him. His punishment was to write the Johnny Appleseed sentence every recess until he had done it perfectly five hundred times.

I caught Alan looking at me a couple of times, but I just turned and looked the other way. Good riddance! I really didn't care anymore.

I was looking forward to going to Miss Latta's office after school every day because I wanted to find out what happened to Jo after she met the cute boy who lived next door. I'd sit there reading until Miss Latta came out to tell me the time was up. On Friday, she let me take the book home.

Cousin Adele and my mother were waiting for me. Both of them were dressed up and ready to go.

"Remind me to get you some barrettes," Adele said when I walked in the door. "How can you see with hair falling in your eyes?"

"If Hope cries, give her apple juice," my mother explained. "It's in a bottle in the refrigerator." I nodded. "I just put Hope in for her nap and she probably won't wake up before we get back. Do you know where the clean diapers are? If you have any problems, your grandmother is home. Do you think you'll be all right?"

"For God's sake, Eleanor! She's almost twelve. Let's go," Cousin Adele said, tugging down her girdle.

"I know what to do. I'll be fine," I insisted.

So there I was baby-sitting. Big deal. I checked on Hope. She was asleep. I poured myself a glass of milk and got a box of doughnuts out of the bread box. I settled down on the couch with my book. Jo's sister Beth had just gotten scarlet fever when the phone rang. It was a lady with a message for my grandmother, so I ran upstairs and told Bubbie that the date of her meeting had been changed. I came down and read some more, and just where Beth became delirious, the doorbell rang. It was Frances with Bandanna.

"Come on in." My mother hadn't said anything about not seeing friends.

"Can I bring the dog in?" Bandanna sat there with a red scarf around his neck and his tongue dangling out of his mouth.

"Is he housebroken?"

"Most of the time," Frances said. She didn't sound too sure.

"Do you think he'll make a mess or not?"

"He's only five months old." Frances reached over and patted him on the head. Sitting down, the dog was already up to her waist.

"I think he better stay out. My mother has a thing about dogs."

"Then I can't come in," said Frances. "If he gets loose, he'll run away, and my mother doesn't like it if he stays out all night."

"Then bring him in." The two of them followed me into the house.

"If he has an accident, I promise I'll clean it up." Frances sat down on the couch and the dog sat down next to her so she let go of his leash. "Guess who I saw in the schoolyard on the way over here?"

"Who?"

"Guess."

"Alan and Joyce making out." I guessed the worst first.

"You're half right. Alan. Can I have a doughnut?"

"Go ahead. What was he doing?"

"Playing ball."

"So?"

"So he asked me where you were." The dog got up and

walked out of the room, but I was too interested in Frances's story right then to say anything.

"What did he say?"

"He said, 'Where's Julie?' " I could hear the dog slurping out of the toilet bowl.

"What did you say?"

"That you were probably home."

"Then what did he say?"

"I don't know. He said something, but Bandanna saw another dog and dragged me down the street so I couldn't hear."

"What did it sound like?"

"I don't know. I was yelling at the dog. Would your mother mind if I ate the last doughnut? My mother doesn't buy this stuff."

"If you're not worried about getting obese, go ahead. But you can't eat anything until you tell me what he said."

"If you want to know so bad, go ask him yourself."

"I'd rather die." Frances didn't say anything. She was eating the last doughnut. "Do you think he's still there?"

"Probably. I got the feeling he wanted you to come over."

"Too bad for him. I'm not going."

"OK," said Frances. What did she care? "Do you know where the dog is?"

"Did Alan look mad?"

"I thought you were the one who was mad."

"You'd be mad, too, if he wanted you to drop dead."

"I told my mother what Miss Latta said and she doesn't

think you need to forgive and forget. She thinks you and Alan are even."

"What do you think Alan wants to talk to me about?"

"How do I know?" Frances stood up and brushed the crumbs off her lap. "Make up your mind if you're coming or not. If you are, we better go now because the dog hasn't done you-know-what. Where did he go?"

"I'm not talking to Alan, but I'll walk you home, OK?"

Frances called Bandanna and the dog came shuffling back into the room. We checked the kitchen on the way out and he didn't seem to have chewed anything or gotten into the garbage. I wiped up the drops around the toilet so you couldn't tell he'd been in the bathroom. When we left, there wasn't a trace of him.

Good thing, because my mother was only prejudiced against two things and she hated both of them with a passion.

Being on time and dogs.

CHAPTER TWENTY-ONE

Ride on a Ferris Wheel

*B*andanna had to sniff under every bush so we walked pretty slowly. By the time Frances and I got to the schoolyard, I could see Alan tossing a ball around with some fifth-grade boys. He was standing with his back to us, waiting for someone to throw him the ball. Then he turned around and looked surprised to see us.

"What's your dog's name?" he asked Frances.

"Bandanna."

"Does he do any tricks?"

"He bites," I said. Just like a Langer. I didn't even say hello, but neither did he.

"Good dog! Good boy!" Alan stuck his baseball glove under the dog's nose so Bandanna could smell it. "See! He doesn't want to bite me."

"You wanna bet?" I said.

"Dogs don't attack without a reason." He rubbed the dog between the ears.

"You'll never know the reason."

"Well, what was the reason?" Alan asked, looking right at me. Somehow we weren't talking about dogs anymore. I got confused. I didn't know how to answer.

"He's a good watchdog," Frances said. "You should hear him bark when somebody comes to the door."

"What did you think you were going to do, collect my life insurance?" Alan asked me. He sounded angry.

"You don't have to make a big thing out of it. I didn't even hurt you."

"You hit me so hard I thought I was going to be the first man on the moon. I still have a lump."

"You do?" said Frances, eyes wide. "Just from an umbrella?"

"Go ahead and feel it."

Frances switched Bandanna's leash to her left hand and touched the spot Alan pointed to. "You do have a bump."

"You want to feel it?" Alan asked me.

"I'll take Frances's word for it."

One of the boys threw the ball and it rolled right past us. Bandanna took off like a bullet. The leash snapped out of Frances's hand.

"I better get him," Frances said, as the dog disappeared around the side of the school building. All the boys were running like crazy. I guess they figured Bandanna would never give the ball back.

"Why did you hit me?" Alan demanded. "Just give me a hint."

"You were making fun of me, or don't you remember?"

"I thought your umbrella looked funny. That's no reason to try and kill me."

The way he said it made it seem as if I'd started all the trouble, as if I'd been mean to him instead of the other way around. What I said next just slipped out because I had to defend myself.

"You didn't even write to me when I was in the hospital."

"I didn't know what to say."

"You could have said, 'Get well soon.' Everybody else seemed to manage."

"And you think that would have made a difference?" He jammed his fist into his glove. I could tell he'd said the words in his head a lot of times before he said them out loud. "You have to be some kind of a jerk to think sending a card changes anything. You think you say 'Get well' and the person gets better, right? Well, you don't know what you're talking about, because whatever's going to happen happens, no matter how many notes or flowers people send. It doesn't make any difference."

"It did to me."

"Well, if I hurt your feelings, I didn't mean to, which is more than you can say about hitting me over the head with an umbrella. I can't believe you did that."

"I'm not bragging about it, you know."

"Well, if you're sorry . . ." he began.

I never said I was sorry. Before I could straighten him out, Frances came back, pulling the dog behind her.

"This damn dog hasn't even gone Number Two yet, but I better get home for dinner or my mother will kill me.

I hope your head goes back to normal, Alan. See you tomorrow, Julie."

Alan and I watched her head off toward her house. Neither of us knew how to get the conversation going again. Alan pulled a key ring out of his pocket and started jingling the keys.

"Are you going to the carnival?" he asked.

"What carnival?"

"The Elks are setting one up at the ball field on Memorial Day weekend. With two Ferris wheels."

"That's a month away. I don't know. I guess I'll go."

"I just thought that if you were going, I'd see you there."

"What about Joyce?" The minute that slipped out I wanted to take it back.

"What about her?" Alan stared at me without blinking.

"She said you were going steady," I lied. Anything to get out of it.

"No, she didn't," he said, "because Joyce is going with some kid from the junior high."

"She is?"

"That's why you hit me, isn't it? You were jealous. I can tell." He looked pleased with himself. He threw the keys up in the air and caught them in his glove. He had a grin on his face as big as the one John Glenn flashed when they picked him out of his space capsule.

"It's getting late. I have to go home." I could feel my face getting red, so I turned and started walking away. I was in the street when Alan yelled something. The boys with the ball had never come back and in that minute, except for Alan, the whole neighborhood was quiet. I heard every word as clearly as I'd ever heard any words in my life.

Alan said, "Just for that, you have to go on the Ferris wheel with me."

The blood zoomed around in my body all the way home, as if my blood cells were on a Ferris wheel, rushing up to my head and down to my toes, then up again. I raced up the walk and skipped up the stairs to the back porch. My heart was rocking back and forth, the way it does when they stop the ride and you're stuck at the tippety top.

When I was just about to open the kitchen door, I remembered.

"Oh, my God," I said.

My mother and Cousin Adele were waiting. I couldn't take my eyes off Cousin Adele's sharp little rat eyes and her sharp little red mouth. The minute I saw her face, I knew what was wrong. I had forgotten all about babysitting for Hope. I looked at my mother for mercy, but she turned away.

"How could you?" she asked, in a voice that didn't even sound human.

"And what animal made a huge mess right at the foot of your mother's bed?" Cousin Adele asked in her sharp little razor voice.

I don't know how I kept on living.

CHAPTER TWENTY-TWO

Regrets

*M*y mother said, "Go to your room. I'll talk to you . . ." but before she'd finished the sentence, I'd run into my bedroom and fallen face down on the bed. I knew my mother would be in to see me as soon as Cousin Adele left. I knew I should be thinking about how I could explain what had happened, but I didn't understand it myself. There were so many questions I couldn't answer.

How could I have left Hope? How could I have forgotten all about my own sister when the only thing she ever did wrong was get born? And that wasn't her fault.

And how could I have hit Alan over the head when he'd never done one thing on purpose to hurt me? What was wrong with me?

I felt jumpy and scared, as if I had a horrible monster inside me that leaped at every chance to come out from where it was hiding and take over. It was angry and jealous and it made me do bad things.

Except I knew there wasn't any monster. It was me.

It hurt to think, but I couldn't stop. A voice in my head wouldn't stop asking questions. Scary questions. Monster questions.

Why did my mother let Cousin Adele pick on me all the time? Shouldn't a mother stick up for her own child?

Why couldn't my parents be together for two minutes without insulting each other? Why did they always have to drag me into the middle?

Would it kill my mother to stop loading the house up with sweets? And was it too much to expect a father to visit his daughter in the hospital? Maybe they were both sorry I'd come home.

I grabbed *Little Women* and read it, even when it didn't make any sense, and I had to read the same words over and over.

"How dark the days seemed now, how sad and lonely the house and how heavy were the hearts . . . dark the days . . . sad and lonely . . . heavy . . . hearts." I made myself read so that I wouldn't think any more.

Finally I heard a knock on the door. My mother came in and stood at the foot of my bed and my father went over and looked out the window. My grandmother came to the doorway and stopped. If she'd come downstairs, things must be really bad.

"How could you have gone out and left Hope alone?"

my mother asked. Her face was white and puffy, like cookie dough, and there was a crease above her nose as if someone had pressed a knife between her eyes. "How could you be so irresponsible?"

"Eleanor, that's an accusation, not a question." My father sounded like a schoolteacher correcting a stupid kid. I could hear my grandmother murmuring, "She's sorry already. She's sorry," right outside the door.

"What if Hope woke up and started to cry?" my mother went on. "What if she started choking? What if she pulled the covers up over her face so that she couldn't breathe?"

"Eleanor, don't make it worse than it is." My father was running out of patience fast.

"What if there had been a fire and nobody knew that Hope was here in her crib? That happens, you know. I'm not making it up. I don't know what's come over you. Julie. What are you trying to do to me?"

"She's only a baby herself," my grandmother answered for me. "She's only a baby."

I could tell my father was at the end of his rope because he started jingling the coins in his pocket. "Do you think you could let the girl get a word in edgewise, Eleanor, because if you're going to get hysterical, I've got phone calls to make."

"Go ahead, you bastard," my mother said, as if I weren't even in the room. "Leave Julie to me. Leave Hope to me. Leave the house to me. Leave everything to me. What happens in this family has nothing to do with you, right?"

"I can bow out with confidence," my father said with a sarcastic smile, "because you're doing such a *great* job." And he walked out.

"I'll talk to you later, Julie." My mother turned so fast she bumped into my grandmother on the way out of my room. "Go ahead in and comfort her, Hessie," she said. "Don't let me interfere with your errand of mercy. Be my guest. I should be used to playing the bad guy by now." Then she was gone.

My grandmother came into the room, holding a white shawl around her shoulders and looking tearful. She sat beside me on the bed and stroked my hair, pushing it back from my face and whispering, "You're sorry already. You're sorry. So you forgot. You're still a baby yourself. It will be all right. You'll see. They'll forget all about it."

The more she tried to make everything all right, the worse I felt. Why should my parents forgive and forget? I wouldn't blame them if they never got over it.

If I were my parents, I would have hated me, too.

The worst thing was, I hated myself so much, I could have saved them the bother.

CHAPTER TWENTY-THREE

The Longest Day

*A*t dinner, nobody said a word about what had happened. We sat there listening to Hope go "lumlumlum" while she ate her jars of baby food. I wanted to say I was sorry, but I was afraid that if I said anything at all, my mother and father would get into another fight. I helped clear the table. Then I went to bed and fell asleep listening to music on the radio.

That night, I had two terrible dreams. In the first one, little people came and started pulling at my pajamas, trying to drag me out of bed. I grabbed hold of the headboard, but they tugged and scratched at my fingers with their nails. When I saw that my mother and father were in the room, I thought they would save me, but my parents didn't move. Then I knew they'd asked the little people to come and take me away. So I let go.

That's when I woke up.

My radio was still on, buzzing with static. I tried to find a station, but it was so late, there weren't any programs. When I switched the radio off, the house was quiet. I wished I could crawl into my parents' bed, but you can't do that if your father sleeps in the nude. I turned on my lamp instead. I was afraid I wouldn't be able to fall back asleep, but I did. I wish I hadn't.

This time I dreamed I was in a hospital. Somebody was being nice and cranking up my bed. Then the bed started folding in half, squeezing my body so I couldn't breathe. I turned to tell the nurse to stop, but it wasn't a nurse. It was my mother. She had putty on her nose so that it had a big hook, and there were wrinkle lines drawn all around her eyes and mouth with a black pencil. I started to scream, but I couldn't because the blankets came up over my mouth. I woke up way under the covers. For a while, I wasn't sure where I was.

I didn't fall asleep again. After a while, gray light came in around the edges of my shades, and not long after that, I heard my father walking around. When I came into the kitchen, my father was sitting at the table in a pair of basketball shorts and an undershirt, eating a piece of whole-wheat toast. He'd made himself a soft-boiled egg the way he likes it, with the white all slimy.

"You mother's got a migraine headache," he said when he saw me. "You'll have to stay home today and help out."

"Where's Hope?"

"I put her in her carriage and wheeled her in by your

mother's bed. If you do what she asks you, she'll manage."

"Where are you going?"

"I'm going to spread fertilizer on the lawn. I've got to get that done this morning before it rains. Then I have to run some errands for your grandmother." My father pushed the corner of his toast into the egg, and when he lifted it out, soupy egg white was hanging off it. He looked over and saw the face I was making. "What are you planning to have for breakfast? A doughnut?"

"I'm not hungry."

"Call me if the phone rings for me," he said, getting up and leaving all the dishes on the table. "Otherwise, you're in charge. Take care of your mother."

When he'd left, I pushed open my mother's door. The curtains were closed and it was dark, but I could still see the outline of my mother's head against the white pillow-case. She had a washcloth on her forehead. She didn't move when I came in. She can't stand to move when her head is pounding. She just whispered, "Hal?"

"It's me."

"Oh." I couldn't tell whether she was pleased or disappointed.

"Can I get you anything?"

"Would you make some toast and then pour hot milk over it? You know how I like it. And will you run this cloth under the cold water?"

I did both those things. I straightened up the whole house, too, and brought my mother the pills she takes. I

127

made my father a hot pastrami sandwich for lunch. It started to rain in the afternoon, so I went around and made sure all the windows were closed. I gave Hope her bottle twice, changed her diapers three times, and put her in her playpen for a while when she got fussy.

I made macaroni and cheese for supper. My father and I ate together, and all through it, he talked about how hard it is to be a success, especially when you have to get ahead in the business world without any help, and how lucky the family was that my father spent his time trying to make money instead of hanging around the house changing Hope's diapers. He got up and took half a head of lettuce out of the refrigerator, and all the time he was crunching away, he gave me a big lecture on eating roughage. I kept waiting for him to mention what had happened, but he never did.

When Frances called after dinner and asked if I wanted to go see Pat Boone in *State Fair* at the Rialto, I told her I had to stay home to take care of my mother. When I got off the phone, my father had gone upstairs. I felt too lonely to stay by myself anymore. I decided to go in and see how my mother was doing. I tiptoed in and sat down on her bed as gently as I could.

"Please, Julie," my mother groaned. "Get off the bed. You're bouncing me." I stood up.

"Aren't you feeling any better?"

"A little. Sometimes I think I get sicker from the medicine than I do from the headache. I'll get up soon."

"You don't have to. Everything's done."

"I have to get up. I can't spend a whole day in bed. Hope's asleep for the night, I think. Why don't you go visit your grandmother?"

"Dad's up there."

"Well, don't just stand there. I'm in no shape to entertain you. Go read the book you brought home from school. I'll get up in about half an hour, I promise."

"About yesterday —" I began.

"Julie, go. This is not the time to discuss yesterday."

"But I'm sorry."

"You're not the only one. Let's talk about this some other time, OK?"

I went into the kitchen and tried to figure out what to do with myself. It seemed as if the day had already gone on forever, but it was only eight o'clock. The rain had stopped, so I went and stood on the porch. There must have been clouds because I couldn't see a thing, not even a single star. Then I heard voices in the yard.

"Shut up," someone ordered. Then there was giggling.

"Who's there?" I called out.

"Who's *there?*" It was a boy's voice.

"It's Julie."

"Hey, it's me, Nick."

I came down the porch steps and went partway down the walk that ran alongside the lawn. Someone switched on a flashlight and shined it in my face.

"Nick? What are you doing here?" I asked.

"Huntin' night crawlers. They're all over the place after it rains. Their tunnels get flooded and if they don't come out, they drown."

"You don't have to tell your folks," someone added. "We ain't hurtin' nothin'."

"Who's that?" I asked.

"That's Ray." Someone turned a flashlight on a boy about six feet tall with pimples all over his face. I'd never seen him before. He looked about seventeen. "Ray's uncle's takin' us fishin' tomorrow," Nick said.

"Hey, don't blame this on me," said Ray. "Comin' here was your idea."

"Is anybody here I know?" I asked Nick.

"This is my brother, Buddy." The light moved over to a kid who looked like a football player. He had a squashed nose, a crew cut, and a broken front tooth. "All these guys are Buddy's friends. They're good kids. You don't have to worry. I'll keep 'em in line." The light clicked off. "You ever catch night crawlers?" Nick asked.

"Sure," I said. "Lots of times."

"You want to help us?"

It was cool and fresh outside, not stuffy like my mother's bedroom. I'd been cooped up all day with no one to talk to, and here was Nick, arms folded across his chest, waiting for an answer.

"OK," I said. "I'll go get my sweater."

CHAPTER TWENTY-FOUR

The King of the Night Crawlers

I found my green sweater in my closet and grabbed the flashlight my father keeps on a shelf in the kitchen. When I came outside, Nick was waiting for me by the edge of the walk.

Our yard runs along the whole length of the house. In front there's a picket fence, but all the other boys were down in the back where there's a wall between us and Winthrop's Market. I could see five or six circles of light moving across the grass back there.

"Your mother know you came out?" Nick asked.

"I don't want to bother her. She's sick," I whispered. "Besides, I don't need permission to go out in my own yard."

"OK. Don't get mad. I was just askin'." Nick started moving into the front yard, keeping his light right in front of his shoes. "I'll find 'em. You grab 'em. You gotta move quick."

"I brought my own flashlight," I said. "I bet I find one

before you do." We started across the lawn toward the street, swinging our lights back and forth in front of us.

"C'mere! Jeez, this one's big as a snake." I turned toward the strange voice. All I could see were flashlights moving toward one corner of the backyard.

"Hey, look at this one," said Nick, right beside me. "I bet he's King of the Night Crawlers."

"It's not a he. They're male and female all in one. The fat pink band in the middle is where the eggs form," I said, staring down at a worm fatter than my thumb and twice as long as my longest finger. It was curled in the grass, and its body glistened a kind of purply-gray. "That's a beauty."

"I got 'em!" Nick lifted the worm in his fist, but the pointy end slipped through the bottom of his hand and stretched out until it was as thin as a pencil. Nick flipped the hanging end back up and opened his palm to show me his catch. The worm went crazy.

"Grab it with the other hand," I said. The worm was whipping around, trying to squeeze out between two fingers. "Don't squeeze it to death," I yelled, but before Nick could get his other hand up, the worm flipped itself into the grass. We both crouched down and started looking, hoping we'd find the worm before the worm found a hole.

"I s'pose you think you could've held on to 'em," Nick grumbled.

"There's a trick to holding on to worms. I've been around them all my life. I'm used to worms."

Nick pointed his flashlight past my left hand. "I think he fell over there."

I moved away from Nick, running the light back and forth across a square patch, looking for that wriggling gleam in the grass, but the worm was probably on the way to China by then. My legs ached from bending over and I was a little off balance, so that when a hand grabbed my collar and stuffed something wet and slimy down my back, I fell onto my hands.

"Now you'll really get used to worms," Nick announced.

"You little rat!" I shouted, standing up. Both my hands were covered with mud. I caught Nick in the beam of my flashlight while I tried to fish the night crawler out with my other hand. I had a pink cotton shirt on under my sweater and the worm was under that, right against my skin. The night crawler must have thought the folds of my shirt were tunnels, because it started heading for home across my back, just out of reach no matter how I stretched. Nick looked so pleased with himself, it made me sick.

"It's not funny!" I yelled at Nick. "If this worm gets squashed, my sweater will be ruined and it's brand-new. Worm blood never washes off, you know. My father's going to kill you!"

"Don't worry. I'll get it out." Nick sounded really sorry. "I'll take it out if you promise not to take a swing at me."

"I swear I won't touch you until it's out," I promised, "but after that, you better start running."

"I'll pull your shirt out in the back so the worm will

fall out on the ground. I won't try nothin' else, I swear. I don't want to make no trouble."

"What 'ja do, you idiot?" Nick's brother came up out of the dark. He had a bottle of beer in his hand. The other boys were right behind him.

"She's got a worm down her back. For a joke." Nick put down his flashlight. "You guys shine some light over here. I'm gonna get it out. Julie, put down your flashlight. I'm not comin' over if you got a weapon in your hand."

I dropped the flashlight without an argument. The worm was traveling right across my ribs in back and the mud where I'd reached under my sweater was itching something terrible. The boys moved in for a closer look. I figured with kids all around him, Nick would have a hard time getting away after the worm fell out. One push and he'd be flat on the ground and I'd be in the house before he knew what shoved him.

I turned and faced the street. Nick came toward me, talking all the way.

"Aw right. Point to where it is, Julie. OK. Now I'm just gonna pull out the bottom of your sweater over that side . . ."

All of a sudden the porch light went on. My shadow and Nick's stretched all the way to the house next door, frozen still, as if we were playing a game of Statues. Boys started running away from the porch. They ran across the front yard and jumped over the picket fence onto the sidewalk. Nick didn't move.

I turned around. The light was so bright, I had to look down. There were beer bottles in the grass.

"Julie, sweetheart, please come in the house," my mother called out.

"Julie, who's that with you?" my father asked.

"It's Nick from school. Nick Sweeney."

"Nick, I think you'd better go home," my father said.

"We wasn't doin' nothin'," Nick protested. "Just foolin' around."

"I think you'd better leave right this second," my mother ordered.

"Go ahead." I gave Nick a little shove on the arm. "I won't get in any trouble, don't worry. They didn't tell me not to come out, and my father doesn't care if kids come in our yard. Go ahead. They just didn't know where I was."

Nick picked up the two flashlights and handed me one. Then he went out the gate. Two boys came out of the shadows by the back of the house and followed him out to the street. When I came up the porch stairs, my mother took my hand and led me into the kitchen.

The worm was heading for my armpit.

CHAPTER TWENTY-FIVE

Bitter Medicine

*W*hen we got into the kitchen, my mother put her arms around me. She gave me a big hug right in the wrong place. I could feel worm blood dripping down my skin.

"Don't! Let go!" I tried to twist away.

My mother stepped back. She had a hurt look on her face.

"Nick put a worm down my back and you squeezed it."

"Oh, my God!" My mother lifted up my shirt and sweater and began scrubbing my back with a paper napkin from the table. "If I wasn't so glad that your father and I got to you in time, this would make me sick." She kissed the top of my head. "Oh, baby, I'm just thankful we got there before anything happened."

"Like what?"

"They were creeping up on you, hon. A few more minutes and God knows what might have happened, but it's all right now. The only thing that matters is that we found you when we did. I think you're getting too big to go out in the yard at night anymore, though. Maybe Adele's right and we ought to move, Hal."

My father shrugged his shoulders. He likes living in his mother's house.

"Nothing bad was going to happen," I said. "Nick's my friend."

"Julie, please. The last thing I want to do is to teach you to be afraid of people, but there's a way to be trusting without asking for trouble. All those boys gathered around you had something in mind, honey, and I don't think it was looking for worms."

"Nothing bad was going to happen. Nick's my friend," I said again. "He doesn't want to hurt me, and not the way you mean. Those boys don't even think about me that way. I'm only eleven."

My mother sat down and pushed the gooey napkins as far away from her on the table as she could. She began rubbing the back of her neck with one hand and I remembered she was sick. I could see she still had her migraine.

"I'm sorry to disappoint you, Julie, but for once your mean mother is not trying to make trouble." She was holding her head funny, as if it hurt her to move it. "It just so happens that your good friend Nick is the one who sent you that vicious little note the day you got back to school, or don't you want to know the truth? Maybe you'd rather be like your father and twist the facts to suit yourself."

"Who said Nick did it?"

"Miss Latta. Mrs. McKay. You can ask them if you don't believe me."

"But how did they find out?"

"Penmanship. *P*'s with a little loop on them. *U*'s that went below the line."

"But why would Nick do that?"

"I guess he was jealous. Jealousy makes people do strange things, you know. I suppose he didn't care how much he hurt you, as long as you ended up angry at Alan. You look surprised, Julie. Sometimes I think you think I'm the only mean person in the whole world."

"I never said that." My body felt stiff and sore, the way it had in the hospital watching the nurses get the needles ready.

"There are some things you don't have to say out loud." My mother's eyes were half closed and she kept looking down at the table. My father didn't move. "Don't you think I know what you and your father think of me? That I'm messy and fat and disorganized. That I don't try hard enough to understand you and take more time . . . as if I could stuff Hope in the closet when she got in the way. Well, it's time somebody straightened you both out. I can't go on this way, without anyone . . ." She stopped. She put both elbows on the table and rested her head in her hands.

"What . . . about . . . me . . . ?" she cried in a little

girl's voice, and all the time she was rubbing her forehead in the places where she presses the cold towels when she gets her headaches. "I can't go on this way. Nobody can give and give and never get anything back."

Her words went inside me just the way the penicillin did. I could feel them burning even when my mother stopped talking. My father was leaning against the wall, biting his lips. I think he was afraid to say anything after the fight he'd had with my mother yesterday.

After a while, my mother lifted her head and looked straight at my father. "I'm going to the Guidance Center, Hal. I want you to come with me."

"Eleanor, there's nothing wrong with *my* mental state," my father said, shaking his head. Then, without saying another word, he put on his jacket and went out.

It wasn't the first time my father had run away from upset feelings. He told me to be tough and stick things out, but he didn't do it himself. The night my parents left me at the hospital, that was the reason I didn't ask if I could wait and say good-bye to my father. I knew he wasn't coming back.

"All right. I'll go alone." My mother sniffed and rubbed her nose with the back of her hand like a little girl. She took a deep breath and her whole body shook. I don't think she remembered I was in the room.

"I'll come," I said.

My mother turned toward me with eyes that looked as if they were shining under water. She reached out her arms and I ran and climbed into her lap. All her softness closed around me and loosened all the stiffness out of my body, as if the shot were over for good.

"I love you," we both said at once. I started to cry, then she did. We dripped tears all over each other's necks and had to wipe them off with clean napkins.

My mother ran the water for a bath and helped me get undressed. She pulled my clothes over my head and threw the pink shirt in the laundry. It turned out that the spots on my sweater were mud, not blood.

So I sat in the tub, scrubbing myself while my mother washed my sweater in the sink. The room was hot and steamy, and when I climbed out, I was sleepy and my mother said her headache was gone.

Words can hurt as much as any needle, but if all the bad feelings get out, it only hurts for a little while.

It's like the nurses said.

Then the medicine starts working.

CHAPTER TWENTY-SIX

Don't Kid Yourself

My mother and I ended up going to the Worcester Guidance Center every Thursday after school, catching the bus at the bottom of our street and walking the whole length of Main Street together. After our appointments were over, we'd stop at a restaurant called Whitman's. My mother would order pie and coffee. I always had a hot-fudge sundae with peppermint-stick ice cream, whipped cream, and nuts. Going to the Guidance Center was sort of a secret, so the only person I ever talked it over with was my mother.

I told her about the way my counselor, Mrs. Epstein, had a way of making the worst things seem perfectly normal.

"When I told Mrs. Epstein I beat Alan up, all she said was, 'You must have been pretty angry.'" My mother didn't say anything because her mouth was full of pecan pie. "She doesn't even think Joyce sounds like a girl who has everything she wants."

"That makes sense."

"She says when I have what I *really* want, it won't bother me when other people get what they want."

"I used to think I knew what I wanted, but then I got it and it wasn't . . ." My mother's eyes filled with tears, but she took a sip of coffee and the tears went away. I don't know why it took me so long to figure out that my mother had her own problems.

"Maybe your father will come with us," she sighed.

"Don't kid yourself again," I said. "He never will."

"Never?"

"Not in our lifetime, anyway."

She smiled. "Four weeks of therapy and you're already smarter than your mother. I can hardly wait for next month's brilliant insight."

That afternoon, when we were riding home, a siren started up in back of us and the bus pulled over to the curb. An ambulance raced by, lights flashing. I squeezed against my mother and she patted my hand. I could tell we were both thinking about the same thing — the night I went to the hospital.

"I thought you hated me because of Hope," I said.

"That's funny. I thought you hated *me* because of Hope."

The man hanging on the strap over us started choking on his cigarette. He coughed his smoke right at the No Smoking sign over our seat, and my mother put her hand over her mouth and nose. Cigarette smoke gives her head-aches.

I pushed open our window to let the fresh air in just as the bus started moving. Pretty soon we came to the Green Street ball field. A long truck was backing into the park and blocking traffic. The bus had to stop again.

The ball field was filling up with men and trucks, and they were setting up a whip, a merry-go-round, and a Ferris wheel. A man up on a ladder was stringing lights, with kids all around him, watching. One of them looked like Alan. A voice called out, "You kids get the hell away from here!" and Nick and his brother came running out from behind one of the tents. Then the traffic started moving again.

We rode the three blocks to our street. I reached up and pulled the rope over the window. Then my mother and I pushed our way out the door.

"All the kids are going to the carnival tomorrow night," I said, as we headed up the street. I crossed my fingers. "Can I go too? Please?"

We walked past two houses while my mother thought it over.

"I don't see why not," she said.

CHAPTER TWENTY-SEVEN

At the Tippety Top

*I*t was just getting dark Friday night when Frances, Shirley, and Gloria came by to pick me up. We each had enough money for ten rides and fifty cents to spend on food. We could hear the music from the merry-go-round as we walked down Green Street, and we could see the carnival a whole block away, lit up like a used-car lot. Before we knew it, we were running. We had to drag Frances by both hands because naturally she'd had to wear her heels.

At first we all just wandered around, looking at the piles of teddy bears, saying hello to kids we knew, trying to figure out the best things to do. We watched some boys throwing hoops over prizes tied to wooden bars. Shirley tried throwing darts at balloons, but she couldn't even stick one in the wall.

All the while, we were keeping an eye out for Alan. He'd called out, "See you tonight, Julie," in the coatroom, right in front of everybody. I was ready to give up hope when Gloria saw him behind the cotton-candy wagon with Donald and Christopher. They were talking to the man who ran the game where you knock over milk bottles with a baseball.

"Let's go get some cotton candy, ladies," said Gloria. "I've been waiting for this all day." We walked up slow and easy. The boys must have been looking for us because the minute Donald saw us, he poked his elbow into Alan's ribs, and they all turned in our direction.

"Hi. You girls ready for the Ferris wheel?" Alan asked. There was a tiny Ferris wheel in the kiddy rides, but the giant was right behind Alan, outlined in red and white light bulbs. It looked as tall as Ash Street School, and it was whirling around so fast all the lights blurred into a shining circle. The seven of us turned and watched it spin. After a while my neck started to ache from looking straight up.

"Well, it doesn't scare me," Gloria said. She fished in her pocket. "I'm going to get some cotton candy."

"You better not eat before you go on the rides," Donald warned. "You'll throw up."

"Cotton candy's nothing but air. It's the greasy hot dogs that get to you," Gloria answered.

"Just my luck, I'll be sitting in the seat right under you when you get sick," Christopher started, but ever since he'd spent a week writing those Johnny Appleseed sentences, he couldn't get Gloria riled up. She figured she'd evened the score.

"Don't you wish it," she said, going off to buy a cone full of cotton candy. When she came back, we all started pulling strands of pink fluff off the cardboard.

"You guys get your own," Gloria yelled, twisting away.

"It's now or never," said Alan. "I've been waiting to ride that Ferris wheel since we watched them setting up yesterday. Has everybody got a ticket?"

We reached into our pockets and pulled out the long streamers of tickets we'd bought at the gate. We stood in line, listening to the men in the booths calling out, "Three balls for a quarter," and "Come try your luck," watching the guy in front of us pinching his girl friend on the behind. Joyce went by with a cute boy, but she didn't see us. She was hanging on his arm and laughing. I really did hope she was having a good time.

Then we got up to the ramp. We could see people's faces as the cars rushed by near the ground. Some of them had their eyes closed and some were laughing. Two girls were screaming their heads off and one boy looked as if his eyes were going to pop out of his head.

"Three of us can go in one car," Gloria said to Frances and Shirley. Everyone knew I was riding with Alan because he was standing right beside me.

"I'm not going." Frances stepped off to the side. "I changed my mind. I don't even like watching."

"I'll keep you company." Shirley backed out right beside her.

"I'm not going up by myself," Gloria protested. "Come on. It's not that bad."

146

"I don't want to leave Frances all alone down here," said Shirley. "Besides, I just remembered how sick I get standing on the fire escape outside Gloria's window. And that's only on the second floor."

"Gloria, you can come up with me," Christopher offered. "That way, if I see you starting to throw up, I can jump out."

"If we were in the same car, you wouldn't have to worry about jumping out. I'd push you."

"I'm just thinking about your safety," said Christopher. "You know what they call this Ferris wheel? The Killer! You need somebody to go on with you."

"You think I'm crazy? I'd never let you that near my cotton candy." Gloria took a big cloud of it and stuffed it in her mouth.

Christopher looked down and scraped one foot back and forth in the dirt. "Julie's going up with Alan so you ought to go up with me," he said finally, " 'cause Alan and me, we got a lot in common."

"Like what, for instance?"

"Well, like Alan got hit over the head and I got framed for a crime I didn't commit, if you know what I mean. I coulda got the electric chair, for all you cared. It seems to me that people who do things like that ought to think about making up for it."

Gloria grinned at Christopher. The last of the cotton candy was melting in her mouth.

"C'mon, Gloria. How many times you gonna make me ask you?"

"Sure I'll go up with you," said Gloria, chewing the last bits off the cardboard cone. "I never said I wouldn't."

"Donald, why don't you go up with Frances and Shirley?" Alan suggested.

"Frances," I asked, "would you feel better if Donald went up with you?"

"No," said Frances.

"I wouldn't feel better even if Pat Boone went up with us," Shirley said. The line started moving.

"You sure?" I called out as the two of them headed off.

"Go ahead. We'll watch," Frances shouted back.

A car stopped and Alan and I climbed aboard. The attendant snapped the bar closed and I grabbed it. I took a deep breath. Alan brushed his hair back from his forehead. The car moved back and up. Then it stopped. Gloria and Christopher climbed into the next car. Alan leaned toward them and the car tipped forward.

"Oh, my God," I said. The words just slipped out. Here we were, still practically on the ground, and I could tell this ride was going to be a thousand times worse than I'd thought, Alan or no Alan.

We went up again. The Ferris wheel jerked to another stop. This time Donald got on.

"Don't move any more than you have to," I said to Alan, trying to make it sound like a joke. "I have to get used to this." The hot dog I'd had for supper was riding around in my stomach.

I counted six more stops before our car reached the top. I could see Frances and Shirley on the ground. They waved their cones of cotton candy and I let go with my left hand and waved back. The car started to rock.

"Oh-oh," I whimpered, grabbing the bar again. We tipped forward and for a minute I thought I was going to fall out headfirst.

"It won't swing so much if all the weight's in the middle," Alan said. His cheeks got flushed, but he moved a little closer. I slid over, too, until the sides of our arms were touching. Music floated up from the ground as we sat there, gently swaying back and forth.

I guess that's what they mean when they say that when you're happy, you feel like you're on the top of the world.

Right before they switch the motor on.